She was in the open. Exposed.

The realization brought a surge of panic, all her senses registering danger. Yet the gathering darkness in the harbor was reassuring. It helped hide her from whatever might be out there in the night. Except the man who loomed over her in the boat, making her nerves jump. Max was too close. But he might not be her worst problem. Something had happened. Something so terrifying her mind wouldn't recall it.

"Trust no one. The enemy will try to stop you."

Someone had drummed that into her, over and over. Someone—but not Max. She knew that much.

His clothes clung to him, outlining a muscular chest and hard thighs. His chiseled face looked concerned, and his voice sounded worried. Or was that just an act?

She pressed a hand to her throbbing head. Pain pounded in her brain, obliterating thought and memory. But she *had* to remember. She knew her life depended on coming up with the right answers. And not just *her* life....

Dear Harlequin Intrigue Reader,

Those April showers go hand in hand with a welcome downpour of gripping romantic suspense in the Harlequin Intrigue line this month!

Reader-favorite Rebecca York returns to the legendary 43 LIGHT STREET with *Out of Nowhere*—an entrancing tale about a beautiful blond amnesiac who proves downright lethal to a hard-edged detective's heart. Then take a detour to New Mexico for *Shotgun Daddy* by Harper Allen—the conclusion in the MEN OF THE DOUBLE B RANCH trilogy. In this story a Navajo protector must safeguard the woman from his past who is nurturing a ticking time bomb of a secret.

The momentum keeps building as Sylvie Kurtz launches her brand-new miniseries—THE SEEKERS—about men dedicated to truth, justice…and protecting the women they love. But at what cost? Don't miss the debut book, *Heart of a Hunter,* where the search for a killer just might culminate in rekindled love. Passion and peril go hand in hand in *Agent Cowboy* by Debra Webb, when COLBY AGENCY investigator Trent Tucker races against time to crack a case of triple murder!

Rounding off a month of addictive romantic thrillers, watch for the continuation of two new thematic promotions. A handsome sheriff saves the day in *Restless Spirit* by Cassie Miles, which is part of COWBOY COPS. *Sudden Recall* by Jean Barrett is the latest in our DEAD BOLT series about silent memories that unlock simmering passions.

Enjoy all of our great offerings.

Sincerely,

Denise O'Sullivan
Senior Editor
Harlequin Intrigue

OUT OF NOWHERE

REBECCA YORK

RUTH GLICK WRITING AS REBECCA YORK

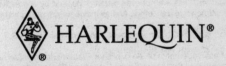

HARLEQUIN®

TORONTO • NEW YORK • LONDON
AMSTERDAM • PARIS • SYDNEY • HAMBURG
STOCKHOLM • ATHENS • TOKYO • MILAN • MADRID
PRAGUE • WARSAW • BUDAPEST • AUCKLAND

ISBN 0-373-22765-5

OUT OF NOWHERE

Copyright © 2004 by Ruth Glick

Visit us at www.eHarlequin.com

Printed in U.S.A.

ABOUT THE AUTHOR

Award-winning, bestselling novelist Ruth Glick, who writes as Rebecca York, is the author of close to ninety books, including her popular 43 LIGHT STREET series for Harlequin Intrigue. Ruth says she has the best job in the world. Not only does she get paid for telling stories, she's also the author of twelve cookbooks. Ruth and her husband, Norman, travel frequently, researching locales for her novels and searching out new dishes for her cookbooks.

Books by Rebecca York

Dear Reader,

A few years ago, I wrote a Harlequin Intrigue book called *Nowhere Man* about a tough, wounded hero named Hunter, who survived a terrible ordeal only because a woman named Kathryn Kelley loved him enough to fight for his life. Recently, *Nowhere Man* was reissued in a volume called *Guarded Secrets*, and I hope the reprint gave a lot of readers the chance to find out about the book because it's one of my personal favorites.

In *Out of Nowhere*, I wanted to do a reverse twist on *Nowhere Man* and write about a tough, wounded, bewildered heroine named Annie, who could survive a terrible ordeal only because a man named Max Dakota loved her enough to fight for her life.

So I've dropped Annie into the middle of a terrifying mess. She's got a vital mission to carry out. The trouble is, she can't remember what it is. And the nasty, bitter people who trained her have drummed into her that she can trust no one. Max Dakota has to work his way under her prickly exterior and prove to her that her only chance of success is with him—and a team from Randolph Security and 43 Light Street, who volunteer to help her. But when they find out the terrible secret she's hiding, the truth challenges even their considerable resources.

You can check out my Web site at www.rebeccayork.com.

Love,

Ruth

Ruth Glick, writing as Rebecca York

CAST OF CHARACTERS

Max Dakota—A secret agent with a past.

Annie Oakland—A woman with no past and no future, who's desperately trying to find her present.

Bert Trainer—As the sheriff of Hermosa Harbor, he loves his job, especially the intimidation part.

Nicki Armstrong—Is her nightclub a front for dirty deals?

Hap Henderson—He keeps an eye on the newcomers to Hermosa Harbor.

Angelo—What role does this shadowy figure from Annie's past play in her present predicament?

Suli—The sister Annie would save—if she could.

Thorn Devereaux—He's got the right credentials to help Annie figure out the mess she's in.

Kathryn Kelley—Can she offer Annie the insight she needs?

Prologue

She had lived a life of terror. A life of deprivation. A life in which nothing had been free or easy. She had learned how to get along in the world any way she could.

But she had never been as frightened in her life as she was now. Because the moment was almost here—unless her pounding heart exploded inside her chest, and she died first.

"You thought you knew what you were getting into," she murmured. "But you were only fooling yourself."

Over the past months she had come to understand that the people holding her captive had placed an impossible burden on her shoulders.

They had trained her in the skills they said she would need. They had crammed a foreign language and a million facts into her head. They had made her spend hours in the gym, honing her body into a fine-tuned machine. They had hardly given her a moment to herself.

But now that the time for departure was almost here, nobody would look her in the eye. Alone, she sat in the molded-plastic chair encased in her tight-fitting one-piece suit.

Underneath that layer of protective clothing, her stomach was churning and her heart was racing.

She pressed her booted feet to the cement floor and looked at the metal door, waiting for one of them to come get her for the final trip to hell.

Her pep talk from Angelo that morning echoed in her head. At first he had sounded almost kind, which was a departure from his usually harsh and frightening tone.

"You are tough," he'd said. "You are smart, and you are as well prepared as a human being can be. But I cannot emphasize enough what I have told you so many times. You must rely on your own skills. You can trust no one."

"But what if I need help?"

"The enemy will try to stop you. Trust no one. They may even be waiting for you."

"How?"

"I do not know. But that could be what went wrong the other times," he'd said in a grating voice. The voice she remembered so well. The Angelo she remembered.

She might have tried to run away. But there had been no place to go. And she knew Angelo would only hunt her down and punish her for her failure of nerve.

So she was here. Waiting for the end of her life as she knew it.

Chapter One

Hermosa Harbor was the perfect town for murder, Max Dakota thought as he breathed in a draft of the sea air, then glanced from his fishing line to the pink-and-orange-tinged sky. Well, at least for a murder investigation.

He was here on the Atlantic coast of central Florida, in a veritable tropical paradise, with nothing to do but figure out who had dumped Jamie Jacobson's body in the marshland outside of town.

The killers had tried to make it look like an accident. A drunken man falling facedown in the swamp and drowning in a few inches of water.

The local police didn't seem too concerned about his death. But Jamie's mother was paying the Light Street Detective Agency to solve the murder. Max hoped she wasn't going to hate the final report, because he was just getting to the good part. And it wasn't pretty.

His small boat drifted along one side of the channel leading from the ocean to the harbor. It wasn't a particularly good spot to catch smallmouth bass. But it was an excellent vantage point to watch traffic on the fifty-foot-high drawbridge over the channel. Probably some of those vehicles were moving drugs from a storage point to dealers who were going to take the stuff north.

Max had been in town for a month, and as far as anyone knew, he was just a guy who'd pulled out of the dot-com bubble before it burst. Since then, he'd been enjoying his early retirement.

Of course, his last name wasn't really Dakota. He had been born Maxwell Daniels, although he hadn't actually used that name in a long time. Max Dakota was one of the aliases he'd picked up during his spy career.

After stowing his fishing gear, he started the outboard motor, then steered toward the bridge, heading back to the marina at a slow pace because this was a high-traffic area.

He'd already learned that Jamie wasn't the only poor jerk who had cashed in his chips in Hermosa Harbor in the past few months. A federal agent had been found floating facedown in the harbor. And a local fitness instructor had taken a dive off his high-rise balcony.

Max was pretty sure Sheriff Bert Trainer was helping to protect the Hermosa Harbor drug trade. At the least, he was willing to look the other way when shipments moved in and out of the community—probably through Nicki's Paradise, the favorite nightspot in town. If the owner, Ms. Nicki Armstrong, wasn't using the club as a storage depot for pot shipments from the Caribbean, Max would eat his baseball cap.

So Max was playing it cool. He'd spent what looked like an indolent afternoon fishing. But suddenly the evening didn't seem quite so lazy. There was something hanging heavy in the humid air. An unsettled feeling of expectation.

Unable to check himself, he looked quickly toward shore. All he saw were small waves lapping against the weeds and a blue heron looking for dinner in the shallows.

He should have been reassured, yet he couldn't shake the feeling of being in the crosshairs of somebody's scope. Getting shot in cold blood was unlikely, he told himself. The other recent murders were all set up to look like accidents.

Still, he knew something was making the skin prickle on the back of his neck. It was like the tension in the atmosphere as a storm was about to break.

It wasn't just a feeling in the air. He was picking up an unpleasant smell, too. Taking a deep breath, he tried to place the odor. Ozone. As though lightning had struck something metal nearby. But he hadn't seen a flash of light.

He was about to chalk up his jangled nerves to the bowl of spicy fish chowder he'd eaten for lunch, when a deep rumbling sound made him jump.

Then in front of him, a wavering pattern of light crackled across the darkening sky.

His mind registered the sequence. Thunder first, then lightning. "That's the wrong order," he muttered.

Bursts of brightness danced rapidly back and forth in the sky, illuminating the bridge, then the clouds, then the bridge again.

He'd never seen anything quite like it. While he watched, a car whizzed past, as though the driver was anxious to get away from the strange phenomenon.

His gaze was fixed in that direction when he saw something else. A person—a woman, judging from her slender, curvy body. From where he sat, it seemed as if she had materialized out of the light show. Wearing what looked like a cyclist's outfit and a helmet, she seemed to be poised on the rail of the bridge. Or just above the rail, which was, of course, a physical impossibility unless somebody he couldn't see behind her was holding her up.

Was she planning to commit suicide? Or was one of the lowlifes in town standing out of sight, getting ready to push her off?

As she clawed at her helmet and flung it away from her, the thought flashed through his mind that the drug trade in Hermosa Harbor was about to claim another victim.

Straining his eyes, he struggled to get a better view of what was going on up there—just as she went flying over the edge and into the water.

An exclamation sprang to his lips, even as he opened the throttle of the outboard motor and headed toward the spot where she'd plunged like a rock into the dark water.

By the time he got there, half a minute later, he saw only a circle of spreading ripples. Turning in all directions, he scanned the channel for some sign that she'd come back to the surface. But he saw nothing in the twilight.

He pulled near her point of entry and cut the engine. Could he find her down there? Probably not, but he knew he had to try. Kicking off his shoes, he reached for his belt buckle and skinned his pants down his legs. After dragging in a deep breath, he dived.

The water was relatively clear, and the lights from the bridge penetrated partway into the darkness. Still, he could see only a few feet in front of his face as he plunged downward, thinking that all he could do was give it his best shot.

He was a good swimmer, and he kept up his surge toward the bottom, his powerful legs kicking, his hands reaching out in front of him and cutting through the water. But he knew that he couldn't stay below much longer. Just as he was about to turn and kick for the surface, his fingers brushed against something that wasn't rock or mud.

It was the woman, lying still as death on the channel bottom. He scrabbled at her slick, one-piece suit but found nothing he could grab on to.

His lungs were near bursting, and he had to fight the impulse to breathe in what would be a lungful of water.

Then his hand touched a strip of fabric. A belt, he surmised as he scraped his way underneath the webbing and closed his fingers around it. Kicking for the surface, he dragged the woman's limp body with him, fighting the fuzzy feeling that threatened to overwhelm his brain.

Finally he broke into the twilight and greedily dragged oxygen into his lungs. He shifted the woman to her back. Slipping his arm under her breasts, and taking a couple of deep breaths, he turned to look at her. She floated unmoving on the surface, a sleeping mermaid, her hair streaming out behind her like strands of blond seaweed.

The boat had drifted toward the shore, and he struck out, dragging her into the shallows where he could stand on the muddy bottom. With an effort, he lifted her into the boat, then hoisted himself over the edge.

After the exertion of getting her out of the water, he wanted to throw himself onto the seat and lie there panting. But he knew her need was greater than his. He was still breathing. She was pale and lifeless.

She looked childlike, although he guessed she was in her mid- to late twenties. And she took care of her body. The flesh he'd felt when he handled her was solid.

Grasping her by the shoulders, he turned her facedown over one of the seats. Then, hunching over her, he pounded on her back.

He didn't know how long he worked on her, expelling the water from her lungs, while his own breath sawed in and out.

It felt like an eternity before she coughed and said something he couldn't quite catch.

"Thank God," he muttered in answer to those first stuttering breaths.

He rested on his haunches as she pushed herself up, then flopped onto her back. The suit she wore was molded to her skin, showing him every detail of her body as if she was naked. He saw that her shoulders were broad for a woman, her breasts medium-size with nipples puckered from her dunk in the cold water.

Moments ago he'd been working frantically to get her breathing again. Now he was conscious of his own state of undress. His wet shirt was plastered to his chest, and his briefs clung obscenely to his lower body.

The woman's eyes zeroed in on him. In the last rays of the setting sun, he couldn't tell their color. But he went very still, caught and held by the intensity he saw there.

Her eyes were large and slightly almond-shaped, their dark lashes standing out against her pale skin. Her face was oval and beautiful in a strange, exotic way.

He couldn't be sure of her nationality. He wouldn't be surprised if she was part Native American or part Asian, although neither of those would account for her wheat-blond hair. It could be dyed, of course, but he saw no suggestion of dark roots.

She seemed to be one of those women whose mixed heritage added up to a very fortunate combination of features. Coming back from the brink of death, she should have looked bedraggled, yet he sensed a super-charged energy coming to life within her.

"Are you okay?" he asked. It was a simple question. But he was startled by the tension gathering inside himself while he waited for her answer.

SHE BLINKED, staring up at the large, dark-haired man who had spoken to her, trying to focus her gaze on his face and her mind on his words. His eyes were light, his nose narrow, his jaw tense. He wasn't a type she had seen often. He had said something, asked a question. He wanted to know how she felt. If she was well.

His voice was interesting. Slow and rich. She liked it. But she knew the words were more important than the way he spoke, and she considered what she might say—even while she desperately scrambled to come up with an answer to the question.

Truthfully, she felt as if she'd been punched in the chest by a giant fist. Her skin prickled and her lungs burned as though she'd been running fast and hard for hours, and her hair was wet, and hanging limply against the sides of her face and neck.

What had happened to her? A sudden spasm racked her, and she coughed, feeling the muscles of her chest protest.

But she welcomed the pain because it pulled her mind away from the raw, hot fear that suddenly welled inside her with the pressure of lava building up inside a volcano about to erupt.

In an effort to control the awful surge of panic, she focused on breathing slowly and evenly. Slipping her hand along the bench where she sat, she grasped the rigid edge, feeling it dig into her skin.

In the gathering twilight, she tried to get a better look

at the man who hovered over her. He was wearing a brightly printed shirt with palm trees and flowers. Both the shirt and his hair were wet.

The fabric clung to his body, outlining hard muscles. As her gaze traveled downward, she focused for a moment on the outline of his sex, thinking it impressive. Embarrassed that she was even noting something so personal, she jerked her gaze lower, seeing the droplets of water that still clung to the dark hair on his powerful legs and thighs.

He had been in the water. With her, she presumed. In fact, when she turned her head, she saw that she was sprawled in the bottom of a small boat in a river.

In the open.

The realization brought a fresh surge of panic. She was in the open. Exposed.

All her senses registered that danger. Yet the gathering darkness was strangely reassuring, because it helped to hide her from whatever might be out there in the night.

Except from the man who loomed over her, dominating the environment, making her nerves jump. He was too close. But he hadn't made any threatening moves. And he might not be her worst problem. Something had happened. Something so terrifying that her mind would not bring it back.

Had this man thrown her into the water? Or fished her out? When no concrete memories surfaced, fear clawed at her again. She heard a warning echo in her head: *Trust no one. The enemy will try to stop you. Trust no one.*

Someone had drummed that into her. Over and over. She could hear the speaker's voice in her mind, but it was impossible to bring his face into focus. Yet the words were as much a part of her as her hair and skin. Someone had said them, and not the man in the wet clothing. She knew that much.

Her gaze flicked to his face again. He looked concerned. And he had sounded worried about her. But that could be a deception, because he could be the enemy.

She raised her hand, pressed it against her throbbing forehead. Pain pounded through her brain, obliterating thought, obliterating memory. But she *had* to remember, *had* to figure out what was going on. She knew her life depended on coming up with the right answers. And not just *her* life.

Holding her body still, she surreptitiously tested the muscles in her arms and legs. They seemed strong. She hoped the impression was not simply wishful thinking.

IN THE GATHERING DARKNESS, Max tried to read the young woman's expression. When she said something that was too low for him to hear, he leaned forward, struggling to decipher her words, but all he caught was the lilting tone of her voice.

"Are you okay?" he asked again.

She didn't answer, and he added, "I'm Max Dakota. I fished you out of the drink."

"Fished…you…out of the…drink," she repeated hesitantly as though trying out a collection of completely strange words.

Well, that had been a pretty flip way to put it, he conceded, as he cleared his throat and tried another question. "What's your name?"

She didn't answer, only continued to regard him as though he was the one who had dropped off a bridge and into the Hermosa Harbor channel.

He wanted to get a better look at her, so he switched

on the camp lantern he'd stowed under one of the seats. The yellow glow showed a woman who was trying to hide her fear. She looked on the verge of tears, and he felt his own chest tighten in reaction.

She seemed utterly alone, utterly defenseless, sitting with her shoulders hunched, wet and bedraggled in the bottom of his skiff.

More than that, he was pretty sure she was in serious trouble, although she might be thinking that she wasn't going to tell him about it.

"I'd like to help you," he murmured, meaning it. When she didn't answer, he added, "It's okay. I won't hurt you."

Of course, she had no way of knowing he was telling the truth. No way of knowing what kind of man he was—beyond the fact that he'd saved her life. Still, the wrong kind of guy could have done it for the wrong reasons.

"Who threw you into the water?" he asked. "Was it one of the thugs from town? Or did you get desperate and decide to take a dive on your own?"

As she seemed to consider the questions, her tongue flicked out, licking across her lower lip, and he followed the motion, caught by her unconscious sensuality.

Well, he assumed it was unconscious, since she hardly seemed in shape for seduction.

"We should get back to my cabin cruiser. You need to get out of those wet clothes."

"No." She moved then, darting forward, catching him by the shoulders. He'd noted that she was in good shape, but her surprising strength took him off guard, and he lost his balance and sat down heavily.

Moments ago, she'd been on the verge of death. A drowning victim pulled from the water just in time.

Now the color was back in her cheeks, her features were intense, and her eyes glittered.

He registered little more than those brief impressions before she took his body in a two-handed grip. Her femininity had caught him off guard. That and her vulnerability.

Now she moved with lightning speed, pulling him off balance, then heaving him up and over the side of the boat as though he were a sack of oranges. In the next moment, he found himself hitting the water and going down for the second time that day, a curse gurgling in his throat as his head went under.

Chapter Two

Max broke the surface of the water sputtering and cursing his stupid willingness to trust. He'd felt sorry for the woman, and she'd tossed him overboard.

He came up in time to spot her leaning over the engine, looking at the controls, apparently trying to figure out how this particular piece of machinery worked.

Her obvious consternation was reassuring. He still had a chance to get his damn property back.

He could have waded through the chest-deep shallows, but swimming was faster. As he stroked toward her, she looked up, alarm clouding her features. Yeah, well, she *should* be worried.

When he reached the boat, she turned and raised her arm, prepared to ward him off.

Instead of going for her, he stood up, planted his feet on the muddy bottom and yanked on the side of the craft, sending it into a violent spasm. To avoid going over the side, the occupant of the boat sat down heavily, her arms flailing.

The torch rolled under the seat and went out. He couldn't see her expression as she pushed herself up and lunged toward him. But he imagined a look of desperation and determination in her eyes as she tried to kick him away.

"Not very ladylike," he growled, ducking, but keeping a firm hold on the boat.

When she flailed out again, he grabbed her foot and pulled. The tactic tipped the boat to its side, sending Miss Kung Fu into the shallow water with him.

He gave her credit for coming up fighting, but he was ready for her tricks this time. He ducked the rigid edge of her hand and countered with a reliable old one-two combination. He'd never socked a woman in the jaw, but he did it now, sending her sprawling backward into the water.

He waited for her to bounce back up, her fists raised. But when she stayed down, a surge of panic knifed through him.

He hadn't saved her life so he could drown her fifteen minutes later. Ducking below the surface, he began searching with his hands extended. He found her quickly and decided not to stand on ceremony, using her hair to pull her up.

After gathering her limp weight in his arms, he held her against his chest, lowering his cheek toward her face.

She was breathing in ragged gasps, and she appeared to be unconscious. Or she was doing a good job of faking it, waiting for another chance to work her way under his defenses.

Well, it wasn't going to happen again, particularly when he thought of what he'd have to put in his report to Light Street.

So he lifted her into the boat again, prepared for some

kind of trick. When none was forthcoming, he scrambled in behind her.

After hesitating for a moment, he used the tie line to secure her hands and feet. When he was sure he wasn't going to be attacked again in his own boat, he started the engine and headed back to the marina.

Halfway there, he decided it might attract a bit of attention if anybody saw him climbing on board his cabin cruiser, *The Wrong Stuff*, with a bound, unconscious woman in his arms.

So he stopped and covered her with a tarpaulin, leaving a tent over her face so she could breathe.

It was fully dark when he reached the slip where his boat was moored. He'd asked for the end of a dock, which provided him some privacy, especially as the craft on his left was owned by a guy who only used it on weekends.

As far as he could tell, he was able to get Miss Kung Fu up the ladder and belowdecks without being seen.

The Wrong Stuff was a custom job, designed for a playboy who enjoyed his creature comforts, which was the role Max had assumed since arriving in Hermosa Harbor. He snorted, thinking his rather down-to-earth parents would have laughed at the status symbol, had they been alive. He carried his visitor through the teak-lined lounge, with its entertainment center and comfortable built-in couches, and below, where there were two cabins and a head. The aft quarters were cramped. But the cabin across the bow was big enough for a double bed and some nice built-in storage furniture. The shower in the head would hold two.

Max hesitated for a moment, wondering where to

take his guest. He decided his bed was be the most logical place, because tending to her in the other cabin would demand the skills of a contortionist.

After laying her on his comforter, he turned on one of the bedside lamps and leaned over her slack body.

"What if I turned you over to the sheriff? Would that be a good idea?" he asked, partly to find out if she was faking her state of unconsciousness.

She didn't answer. Despite her attack in the skiff, the thought of tossing her like a piece of choice meat to Bert Trainer made his stomach knot. For all Max knew, Trainer could have been the one who had ordered her pitched off the bridge.

Driving her to the hospital emergency room was his logical next move. But if she was in trouble, whoever was after her—Trainer or someone else—would find her there and likely finish the job he'd started.

That was a good reason for hiding her here. And there were other reasons, too. The story she had to tell might help him nail Jamie Jacobson's killer. She might even know the amount of dope being moved through Hermosa Harbor. If she trusted him enough to talk. So far, she'd given no evidence that she was going to come clean with him.

But maybe a little TLC would persuade her.

Some deeply hidden part of him liked that plan, even when he knew that trusting this woman might be the biggest mistake of his life.

Yet he kept thinking of an old Chinese proverb—or whatever culture it had come from. When you saved a person's life, you were responsible for him or her.

Nonsense, he told himself with a snort.

The woman who had become his responsibility lay with her eyes closed, but he wondered again if she was faking unconsciousness.

He'd used that ploy on occasion himself—when he'd been trying to avoid inconvenient questions.

He'd called her Miss Kung Fu, but maybe something else would do better. Something that wasn't out of a martial-arts movie.

As he thought about it, his hands were busy pulling off her short, tight boots. When he inserted his finger under the tops, the material gave, and he was able to quickly ease them off her feet.

He held them up to the light, studying the pointed toes and little heels. They looked like leather from the outside, but they were thinner and lighter and very well made. The tops were shaped like cowboy boots. And that brought a name from a Broadway show zinging into his head.

Annie Oakley.

"What do you think, Annie? Is that a better name for you?" he asked, not expecting an answer and not getting one. "At least until you fess up and tell me something different. And by the way, why don't you help me sort out the good guys and the bad guys in Hermosa Harbor?"

After setting the boots on the floor beside the bed, he looked back at the woman, who lay with her eyes closed.

He'd brought her to his boat and laid her on his bed. Were those actions just more of the sort of risky behavior he'd engaged in after he'd come staggering back from San Marcos without Stephanie?

He hadn't really cared if he lived or died, so he'd taken some outrageous chances. Like when his former employer, a top-secret spy organization called the Peregrine Connection, had needed an informant sprung from a covert prison in Afghanistan. He'd volunteered to go in and get the guy out. And he'd succeeded—leaving half-a-dozen dead guards scattered around the prison compound. He'd been prepared to take on other assignments with similar risks, when another former Peregrine operative, Lucas Somerville, had come down to the agency's secret headquarters in Berryville, Virginia, to see him.

Lucas had acted as if he'd just wanted to find out how Max was doing. But Max suspected the director, Addison Jennings, had suggested the visit.

Lucas, who now worked for Randolph Security, which was affiliated with the Light Street Detective Agency, had persuaded Max to give up the high-risk spy business. Which had probably saved his life.

Since joining Light Street, he hadn't been operating at quite such a death-defying level. Still, he recognized the impulse to put his own safety at the bottom of his priorities.

Switching back to practical matters, he turned his attention to his prisoner's condition. He was no doctor, but he'd had plenty of emergency experience. Methodically, he checked her vital signs as best he could. Her chest rose and fell in a steady rhythm. It seemed as if she was breathing normally. When he pressed his fingers to the artery in her neck, the rhythm of her pulse felt normal. As he untied her bonds, Max wondered if she was suffering from shock.

He'd seen this kind of reaction when he'd come into a village in San Marcos after rebels had swept through the area, killing men, women and children. Some of the residents were unconscious—even though they had no injuries. He figured what had happened was too terrible for them to face, so they'd gone into some private world where nobody could reach them.

Was that what had happened to Annie?

SHE LAY VERY STILL, considering her options now that the man had untied her.

Her head was still pounding. But she had worse problems. Despite the soft surface under her body, she felt as though she was being sucked into a black hole in space, unable to stop herself and unable to figure out where she was going to land. In the past or the present. Or the future.

The endless void was terrifying. So she focused on the present, on each separate second of her existence, all her effort going into not letting the man know that she was now aware of what was going on around her.

When she'd tried to escape, he could easily have killed her, and she should probably count herself lucky that he'd only knocked her unconscious.

Of course, he had his reasons for sparing her life. She gathered from what he had said that he thought she had information that would be useful to him. The problem was, she would not be able to tell him anything he wanted to hear.

Through a screen of lashes, she studied him, thinking that she had been lucky to get him out of the small boat in the first place.

But what kind of personality lurked behind those icy blue eyes? Did they ever turn soft? Or was he always prepared for trouble? Finding out was vitally important.

She was lying on a wide bed in a small bedroom. Given that the surface under her rocked gently, she was pretty sure he had carried her onto his boat. He had told her he was going to do that.

Now she could see him much better than in the small craft on the river. He looked tough. Like a cop. Or the chief of a tunnel gang. She tried to hang on to that interesting thought, but it skittered out of her mind as quickly as it had come, and she was left with the man between her and the door.

She wanted to cringe when he sat down beside her on the edge of the bed, but the discipline she had learned kept her lying still and focusing on small details. His eyebrows and lashes were dark. His nose and chin were what she might have called aggressive. When he pressed his lips into a straight line, he looked as if violence was his natural mode of operation. Then they would soften, and she could imagine them breaking into a full-fledged smile. If he ever had anything to smile about.

A day's growth of dark stubble covered his cheeks and chin. It did not completely hide a thin line below the left corner of his mouth. He'd been cut, but the scar was old. Another one on his forehead looked more recent.

Suddenly it seemed vital to find out what had happened to him. But he interrupted her thoughts with another question.

"I've been calling you Annie. Do you have a name?"

The question made her stomach clench and a cold sweat break out on her skin. She beat back her fear with all the considerable determination she possessed. She could not afford to let her emotions take over from her brain. If she knew anything, she knew that much.

"I'm going to check your head," the man said.

Gently, oh, so gently, he sat her up, leaning her against his chest. She might have struggled, might have tried to push away, but the warmth of his body seeped into hers and was strangely comforting. Which was no proof she could trust him, she told herself again as he began to probe through her hair, his large fingers feeling her scalp, abrading her nerve endings.

"No lumps," he said, his voice sounding gruff. "No depressions and no places where your scalp has been cut."

The information eased her mind—at least as far as head injuries were concerned.

Carefully he laid her back on the bed. Her eyes were still closed, but there was something else she must tell him. She was hurting, and she needed to know if the injury was serious. Could she do that without revealing she was awake? Slowly she raised her hand, touching the front of the one-piece suit she wore, groaning softly.

"WHAT'S WRONG? Something hurts?"

Her lips moved. "Umm." The sound was barely audible.

He watched as she rolled her head on the pillow, then plucked again at the fabric covering her breasts. It was part of a one-piece suit, tight-fitting and made of some space-age fabric. Not a cycling outfit as he'd first thought. More like something an astronaut might wear. Hardly clothing he'd expect to see on the street in Hermosa Harbor.

The fabric was blue with a slightly reflective layer on top. But when he followed the motion of her hand, he saw that the material across her chest was discolored.

In fact, now that he gave it a good look, it appeared scorched. If her skin was burned underneath the garment, then she must be feeling it.

There was no obvious opening at the front of the suit.

"How do you get out of this thing?" he muttered.

She didn't answer, apparently back to pretending obliviousness to her surroundings. If that was the way she wanted to play it, he thought, then she could damn well take the consequences.

After hesitating for a moment, he skimmed his hand up the bodice, very conscious of the swell of her breasts. At the neckline, his fingers located a hidden zipper. When he lowered it five or six inches, he found that the skin of her chest was red. It looked as if she and the suit had, indeed, been burned, and the shiny fabric had protected her to some degree. But not entirely.

He thought of the lightning he'd seen crackling around the bridge when she'd first appeared. That could have been the heat source. But he was pretty sure if it had struck her, she'd have a lot worse injuries than what looked like a sunburn.

Still, he knew it hurt. "You need something on that," he said.

When he'd first come down to Florida, he'd scorched

his hand while working on the boat's engine, and he still had the cream he'd used to soothe the injury. It was in the drawer beside the bed.

Holding up the tube, he said, "Here's some salve for the burn. Do you want to put it on yourself?"

She remained silent, so he reached for the zipper and lowered it another few inches, exposing more skin. He'd hoped she was wearing a bra, but no such luck. He could see that the inside curves of her breasts were red, along with the flesh in the center of her chest.

Opening the tube of cream, he spread some on his fingers, then reached to rub it onto her injured flesh. Just like a doctor treating a patient, he told himself. She had let him know she was in pain, and he was easing her discomfort. Unfortunately, touching her chest with his fingers didn't feel like a medical procedure.

Her skin felt warm and smooth, silky, as he gently spread on some of the salve.

She made a small sound, and he couldn't tell if he was hurting her or easing the discomfort.

He'd tried to get her to take charge of the first aid. But apparently she wasn't capable of doing the job herself. Or was she deliberately letting him do it?

He couldn't help thinking it would be an interesting change of tactics. This woman had fought him like a tiger. She'd tried her best to steal his skiff and get away. He should be treating her like a prisoner of war, instead, he was touching her intimately, and it was turning him on.

Too bad he couldn't control the sensations being transmitted from the nerve endings of his fingertips.

Looking down, he saw her nipples poking against the

fabric of her suit, telling him he wasn't alone in his reaction to the intimacy. Or was he simply observing some kind of involuntary physiological reaction?

He dragged in a sharp breath, wondering what the hell to do now. Time seemed to have stopped, leaving the two of them in an airless bubble where it was impossible to draw a full breath.

On an intellectual level he knew he should pull his hand away. Finally he was able to make his muscles work, feeling as if he'd achieved some kind of monumental victory as he pressed his palm flat against the mattress.

Once again, he looked at her face—just as her eyes snapped open.

Seeing them was a shock. Her irises were dark, impossibly dark for someone with such blond hair, he thought in some corner of his brain. But they went with the oval shape.

She looked down at the front of her suit, then quickly pulled the edges of the fabric back together and worked the zipper.

"I was putting salve on your burn," he said, wondering if either one of them would accept the explanation.

She didn't seem to be listening to him, though. She was staring at the bulkhead behind him, her brow wrinkled as though she was trying hard to remember something important—something just beyond her grasp.

Her gaze found his, and her lips moved again. At first, no words came out. Then she asked, "Where…am I?"

Her lilting accent sounded Scandinavian. She was

blond enough to hail from the land of the midnight sun, but the dark, almond-shaped eyes were an anomaly.

The almost pleading look in those eyes snapped his attention back to the question she'd asked. "I've brought you to my boat," he replied. "You're safe here."

She nodded, but he wasn't sure she believed him.

"Tell me your name," she demanded.

He repeated what he'd told her earlier. "Max Dakota." Apparently she was having short-term memory problems.

"Is that your real name?" she asked.

He laughed. "Odd question."

"*Is* it?" she asked, her tone low and urgent, as though the fate of the world depended on his answer.

"Yeah," he replied, because he had an obligation to protect his cover. He'd had no trouble putting the name around since coming to Hermosa Harbor. Strange that he should want to tell this woman something different. But he didn't have that luxury.

"What are you doing here?" he asked.

She gave a quick shake of her head, and it looked as if she was on the verge of tears again. He wanted to reach out and gather her close, comfort her, but he restrained the impulse.

"Why did you kick me out of the skiff?" he asked, instead.

"The what?"

"The little boat."

"I thought you were going to hurt me."

"I pulled you out of the water and got you breathing again. Why would I hurt you?"

"People—men—take advantage of the weak."

The absolute conviction of her words made his throat clog painfully. "I don't," he said, punching out the words.

"You tied me up."

So she remembered that.

"What choice did I have? You hit me and kicked me and threw me in the water. You would have left me sputtering there if you'd been able to start the engine, wouldn't you?"

She didn't answer, but he saw from her eyes that he'd described her thoughts pretty well.

"I don't suppose you'd promise not to try something like that again…"

She had taken her bottom lip between her small white teeth. Releasing it, she said in a low voice, "I am sorry I attacked you. I will not do it again."

Max noticed she hadn't promised not to try to get away again.

"Did somebody push you off the bridge?" he asked.

"The big bridge?"

"Yeah. You were up there before you went into the water."

"I was?" Her eyes grew large.

"Are you mixed up with Bert Trainer?"

"What is that?"

"Not what. Who. Sheriff Trainer."

"I…do not think so," she answered, sounding unsure.

He wanted to ask her more, but neither of them was in shape for that now. His own damp clothing made him realize she was probably feeling pretty uncomfortable, too.

"You should get out of that suit you're wearing," he said. "You can put on something of mine."

Quickly he got off the bed and turned to the storage unit at the end of the room, debating what to bring her. He pulled out a pair of his gym shorts and one of the Hawaiian shirts he'd been wearing since he'd arrived in town.

Underwear was another consideration. Of course he couldn't offer her a bra, and he was confident she wouldn't want to wear his cotton briefs. If she stayed with him, he'd have to buy her undergarments.

Thinking he was getting way ahead of himself, he switched to another problem. Shoes. A pair of flip-flops he'd found on the boat would have to do, since her little cowboy boots would look rather comical with the shorts and shirt he'd picked out.

After he set the outfit down on the foot of the bed, she sat with her head bowed for several moments, then raised her eyes to his, searching his face as though trying to find out something she hadn't known ten seconds earlier.

"Why are you being nice to me?" she asked in a thin voice that barely carried across the small space between them.

Chapter Three

Once more the woman's apparent vulnerability tugged at Max. And once more he wasn't sure how to answer. He settled for, "You're obviously in trouble."

A small shudder seemed to go through her. "Yes. But I am asking about you."

Well, she'd gotten right to the point. "Call me a knight in shining armor."

He watched her chew that over. "What does that mean?" she asked after several seconds.

He tipped his head to one side. "It's a pretty common expression. It means a man who comes to a woman's rescue. But if you're from some other country, you might not have heard it."

He'd given her an opening, but she didn't take it. She was hugging her arms across her chest, looking as if she was holding herself together.

He sighed. "Okay, so you don't want to tell me about yourself. But you should change your clothes. Maybe shower first. I'll show you where to find the head."

Looking frustrated, she opened and closed one hand. "I do not know that word, either. Well, I know the word, but I thought it was this." She tapped her fingers against her temple.

He shrugged. "That's the good old English language for you. There are all kinds of strange word uses. In this case, the head is the bathroom. That's what we call it on a boat," he explained, knowing a lot of people weren't familiar with the nautical terminology.

"The bathroom. Okay." She dragged in a breath and let it out, apparently steadying herself before climbing off the bed.

He held out the tube of burn salve. "Put more of this on after your shower."

"Okay."

Stepping into the companionway, he waited for her to follow. As she took a few steps after him, the shrill sound of a smoke alarm pierced the stillness.

"Damn," Max muttered. Some fool on a nearby boat was probably grilling steaks in the galley again when he should be using the open deck. "Let's hope they get the battery out of that damn thing before it splits our eardrums."

He had turned to deliver the observation to his guest when he noticed the expression of utter and complete horror on her face.

What sounded like a curse sprang to her lips...well, not any curse he'd ever heard. Something like "Carp!"

In the next second, she threw herself to the deck, holding her hands over her head and hiding under them.

Max stared down at the woman. Though she'd fought him fearlessly in the boat, the piercing wail of a smoke detector had reduced her to a quivering mass of terror.

He hunkered down beside her, gathering her close, wrapping his arms around her and rocking her gently. He stroked her shoulders and murmured low, reassuring words.

She might have pulled away, but she stayed where she was, still shivering violently.

"It's just a smoke alarm," he soothed. "On one of the other boats. Not here."

"No, it is death," she choked out. "Death."

He pressed one of her ears to his shoulder and covered the other one with his hand, at the same time wedging her face against his chest, waiting out the high-pitched sound. Finally, inevitably, it stopped.

Still, she trembled against him, and he bent his head, caressing her cheek with his lips, trying to soothe her as best he could.

"It's okay. It's all over."

"I...I saw them...all those bodies...lying there. So many of them. Dead. You could tell that it...it was awful. Their hands were clawing at the air. At their faces. The way they died was awful."

The enormity of her words made him gasp. "Where were you? In a war?"

"I do not know!" The admission sounded like a confession of guilt. "But I have to save them."

She sounded on the verge of hysterics. "It's okay. Everything's okay," he murmured, trying to reassure her. "There are no bodies here. What you heard was just a smoke alarm on one of the other boats," he repeated.

She didn't seem capable of listening to his explanation. Her fingers dug into his forearms, her grip strong and painful as her gaze locked with his.

"No. You have to understand. People will die, I have to stop it from happening. I am here to do that."

Questions bubbled out of him. "How? Who sent you? What do you have to do?"

She shook her head and looked away, breathing

slowly and evenly. Moments before, he'd seen panic grab her by the throat and choke off her breath. Now he knew she was working to conquer it.

He saw her subdue the look of terror inch by hard-won inch. By the time she looked back at him, she had composed herself. "A smoke alarm?" she said, and he realized that she'd heard him, after all.

"Yes. Some jerk is grilling steak in a confined space."

"How do you know?"

"It's happened before. One of the marina residents has had a little too much to drink."

She nodded, and though he wasn't sure she completely followed the explanation, she seemed to accept that the emergency was over.

Max switched back to the previous topic. "Where did you see those bodies? Do you know what happened to them?"

She lowered her gaze, pressed her lips together.

He sighed. "Okay. Go change out of your wet clothing. Maybe you'll feel like talking when you're more comfortable," he said, fighting to keep his voice even.

Opening the door to the head, he looked around, trying to see the room from the perspective of a visitor who had dropped in from the vicinity of the channel bridge. He instructed her on how to flush a toilet on a boat, then warned her not to use too much water in the shower, because he wasn't due to fill the water tanks until next week.

She nodded gravely as he pulled a large towel from a wall compartment and laid it on the sink, along with some essentials he kept around for female guests.

"Here's a brush and a hair dryer. You can plug it in there." He pointed to an electrical outlet on the wall.

"Yes. Thank you." She sounded eager to be alone, so he departed quickly.

Back in his cabin, he undressed and washed, using the sink in the corner, then pulled out another tropical shirt and navy Bermuda shorts. As he took the wet outfit to the deck and hung the items over the back of a chair, he thought about knocking on the door of the head and asking Annie Oakley to toss out her suit. He wanted to get a look at it. But he figured he'd have a chance to do that later.

In the galley, he opened the refrigerator and looked inside. After the evening's activities, he was hungry. Probably his guest was, too. What would she like to eat?

He laughed softly. He was certainly being accommodating to a woman who'd thrown him in the channel and tried to steal his boat. But there was something about her that tugged at him. She was in a jam, but she insisted on playing by her own rules. Much as he didn't want to have an emotional response to her, he couldn't help himself.

Deliberately he turned his attention to dinner. He was a good cook. When he and Steph had been between assignments, he'd been the one to spend time in the kitchen.

Despite the challenges of a small galley, he'd duplicated some of the fancy meals he'd eaten in restaurants. The day before he'd made some fettuccine Alfredo.

He'd serve her that, along with a mozzarella, tomato

and avocado salad he'd enjoyed on a London assignment.

He was getting the meal ready when he heard someone walking along the dock.

The footsteps stopped, and he looked through the window.

Damn. Hap Henderson was out there, his belly pouching out the front of his knit shirt.

Hap was in his late forties, Max judged. Because his hair was thinning on top, he almost always wore a captain's hat.

He lived on one of the other boats in the marina, a cabin cruiser that wasn't quite as luxurious as *The Wrong Stuff.* But Max was pretty sure that Hap was involved in the drug smuggling that centered around Hermosa Harbor. Too bad there was no way to prove it yet.

He suspected that one of Hap's duties was to keep tabs on new arrivals in the community. Had he seen the owner of *The Wrong Stuff* bring aboard a visitor wrapped in a tarp?

"Hey, buddy, want to have a beer?" Hap asked through the open window.

"Not today."

"You got something better to do?"

"Yeah. A heavy date."

Hap looked through the window. "Somebody I know?"

"An old girlfriend from up north," Max improvised. "She's down in the head taking a shower."

"Oh. Okay. Maybe we can get together tomorrow."

"She may be staying with me for a couple of days."

Hap made a grunting sound. "Wouldn't want to interfere with your love life, boy," he said before turning and strolling back down the dock.

Max watched him leave, thinking he should warn Annie about nosy old Hap. But then, if she was in trouble with the smugglers, she might already know the guy. Maybe she could impart some of the information Max was missing.

"ANNIE," SHE SAID as she stood with her hands clenching and unclenching. "Annie."

There was a mirror over the sink, but she averted her gaze as she tugged at the zipper of her jumpsuit, opening the front all the way and peeling down the fabric. Her chest was still red, but the salve Max Dakota had smeared on her skin had helped.

The memory made her nerve endings prickle, and she fought to banish the sensation. Her brain must be soft if she had let him touch her like that.

She was not here to enjoy herself with Max Dakota. She was here to...

To what?

The question clawed at her, making her double over at the waist and hug her arms around her middle. She had been trying to put off the moment of truth, but it had snuck up on her when she was not looking.

The image of the dead bodies flashed back into her mind again. She was here to keep them from dying. At least she thought she was. But maybe that was a false memory someone had planted in her brain.

A false memory. That was a drastic conclusion. Yet

she must not discount it. She must not discount anything.

"Carp!" she said, the harsh syllable helping to discharge some of her tension.

Leaning over the sink, she turned on the water and looked at the clear stream. Was it safe to drink?

Thirst made her reckless. Cupping her hands, she gulped down several swallows. It tasted wonderful. Clean and fresh.

When she had her panic almost back under control, she straightened and finished unzipping the suit, then began to pull her hands out of the sleeves.

Moments later, she stood naked in the bathroom— the head, she reminded herself. It was called the head.

The word should not be a problem. She was a good language student. She was already thinking that Max Dakota spoke English differently from the way she did. And she should modify her own speech patterns. Her linguistic skills had been important for this job.

Important for this job. Her hands clenched and unclenched as she fought to grab on to the sliver of memory and pull it into the center of her thoughts. But holding on to it was as impossible as wrestling an alligator.

An alligator. Well, she knew what that was. A dangerous animal she had been cautioned to avoid. They lived in Florida. A place in the United States. She knew that much. So was she in Florida?

When she could not come up with an answer, she turned to the full-length mirror on the wall and looked at herself for the first time. Her heart was pounding so hard she could actually see it making her chest move. But she stood very still, striving for objectivity.

How would she evaluate this woman if she met her for the first time?

Her body was trim, no extra fat. She looked as if she had been training rigorously for this assignment—whatever it was, she silently added.

Trust no one. The warning echoed in her mind again—the only thing she was sure about in a world that was shifting dangerously under her feet. And not simply because she was in a boat.

A small sound rose in her throat as she slapped her palm against her thigh, then winced at the sting of pain she had produced.

She did not know who she was. There, she had admitted it. She did not know what she was doing here. But she knew that a lot of people were going to die if she could not figure it out.

Would Max Dakota help her?

Forget Max Dakota, she told herself firmly. But it was impossible to completely banish him from her mind.

Swallowing hard, she looked back in the mirror, seeing the terror written on her features. With objectivity, she took in other details. Her hair was light. All over.

She had shaved the hair under her arms and on her legs. It felt strange, but she would just have to get used to it.

Again she stopped and tried to hold on to the significance of that thought. Was shaving something new to her?

Pivoting away from the mirror, she turned on the shower and stepped under the spray.

There was a bar of soap in a little rack on the shower

wall, and she picked it up, lathering her hands. The ensuing aroma made her go very still. The soap smelled wonderful. Not just fresh and clean, but like something good to eat.

She had no precise words to describe it. She only knew that it was rich and spicy and a shock to her senses. Lifting it to her face, she sniffed it, then tentatively stuck out her tongue and touched it to the bar.

After the enticing scent, the taste was an unpleasant surprise. But, then, it was not supposed to be food. It was soap. And she did not need to eat it to enjoy it.

Feeling as if she was wallowing in sinful luxury, she lathered her body.

Her right hand stilled when she came to some kind of raised place on her skin under her left arm, toward her back. The area felt tender, and she twisted around, trying to see it. But the light in the shower was dim, and the thing was almost on her back where it was hard to get a good look at it.

So she went on to washing her hair—another sensual experience. The shampoo was even richer and more tangy than the soap. And it made her hair feel so silky she wanted to run her fingers through the strands just for the pleasure of it.

Finally, recalling Max Dakota's warning not to use too much water, she forced herself to turn off the water and step out, then picked up the towel he had left on the sink and began to dry herself.

Again, the experience was amazing. She wondered if she had ever felt anything so soft and absorbent against her skin. The towel was large enough to envelop her, and the fluffy fabric sucked the water away from her body, leaving her feeling wonderfully dry and clean.

How astonishing that such simple things could feel so good, she thought. And even more astonishing not to remember any of them.

She clenched her teeth and reached for the brightly patterned shirt—then remembered the place under her arm that had felt strange to her soapy fingers.

Holding up her arm, she moved closer to the mirror, twisted around, and saw a small blue mark. Seeing it sent a shiver slithering down her spine, like a snake ready to wrap itself around her body and choke the life out of her.

What, exactly, was she looking at?

Chapter Four

Twisting around farther, Annie tried to get a better look at the mark. The color was dark blue, and as far as she could tell, it was some kind of symbol tattooed on her skin. A circle with an X through it.

Experimentally, she touched the blue symbol with the fingers of her other hand. Confirming her impression from the shower, the area was slightly tender, as though the thing had been put on her fairly recently. She pressed, wondering if it was her imagination or if there was something below the surface of the skin under the tattoo.

She pictured herself showing the blue mark to Max and asking him if he knew what it was. Almost as soon as the idea came to mind, she squeezed her hands into fists, fighting the needy feeling rising inside her. Her interaction with the man was warping her judgment. She had to remember that she was on her own.

Probably it was better to get off his boat. But just contemplating that idea made her chest tighten. She felt safe here.

Or was she? Quickly, she gave herself an excuse for staying: it was better to find out as much as she could before she took off on her own.

Still feeling uncertain, she dressed as quickly as possible in the borrowed shorts and shirt. The sandals were not very comfortable, so she left them on the floor.

She was about to leave the room, but at the last minute, she turned to the mirror and gave herself a critical inspection. The clothing she wore looked too big. The shirt hung down to her knees, almost hiding the shorts that played hide-and-seek at the bottom when she moved her legs.

Hide-and-seek. A children's game where one person is "it" and has to locate the others.

The definition had popped into her head. Not because she had played the game, she was sure, but because she had been forced to memorize it.

Why?

Simply contemplating the question made her chest tighten again. Frantically she shoved the question out of her mind and went back to her inspection. Her hair was a mass of tangles. But using the hair dryer and brush Max had offered would fix it.

Snatching up the little machine, she turned it over and over, enjoying the way the smooth plastic felt in her hand. It was like the soap—a foreign object.

When she pushed the tiny prongs at the end of the cord into the receptacles in the wall, then toggled the switch, the thing came to life with a roar in her hand, and she almost dropped it. But when she directed the blast of warm air at her hair, it felt good. She began to work on the long, blond strands, untangling them with the brush.

The simple process seemed to transform her appearance. Tentatively she brushed back the blond cloud, liking the effect of her hair flowing softly around her face.

Would Max like it, too?

With a grimace, she told herself it did not matter how he reacted to her appearance. Still, she thought, if he liked her—liked the way she looked—she might get him to cooperate.

The idea of using her looks as a tactic made her mouth go dry. But she had to leave all options open she knew as she unlocked the door with a decisive click and stepped into the narrow hall.

Greeted by a wonderful aroma, she heard her stomach growl in reaction, and she was glad she was alone at the moment.

Following her nose, she climbed a flight of ladderlike steps and found herself in a room that was comfortably furnished with tailored sofas and chairs and a dark wooden table. She ran her hand over the back of a sofa, entranced by the feel of the fabric.

Max was at the other end of the room in what must be the kitchen. She heard him making a low, contented noise and realized he was singing a song. Something about lovers and guns.

His shoulders stiffened, and she knew he had been listening for her. He turned, a spoon in his hand. She saw his gaze travel over her, from her hair to the baggy clothing he had lent her to her bare feet, then up again.

Suddenly she was conscious that she was naked under the light coverings. Swallowing, she said, "Thanks for the use of the shower…and the hair dryer."

"You're welcome." He gave her a grin. "You clean up pretty good," he said.

"So do you," she answered, thinking that he looked very appealing but no less dangerous in his clean shirt and shorts.

"How do you feel?" he asked.

"Better."

The conversation came to a halt. Scrambling for something else to say, she asked, "Why were you singing?"

He shrugged. "No reason, really. Well, it's from *Annie Get Your Gun.* The Broadway musical that gave me the idea for your name."

"Oh," she answered cautiously. Too bad the reference was totally mystifying. Unlike with hide-and-seek, nothing relevant popped into her head.

She moved farther into the room, drawn as much by the food as by the man. "What smells so good?"

"Fettuccine Alfredo." His tone was casual, but she was pretty sure he was not quite as relaxed as he wanted her to think.

"Umm," she answered.

He looked disappointed. "You don't like it?"

"Oh, I love it!" she lied, wondering what in the name of The Protectors it was.

"Well, I'm starving. Let's eat."

A container of white strands was sitting in the sink, steam rising from the surface. He transferred the strands to a bowl, then added the contents of another pot before forking out portions onto two plates.

"Let me help," she offered, thinking that she had never seen a man perform this work, but wondering what she could do, since neither the food nor the equipment seemed familiar.

"Carry those to the table," he said as he brought more food.

She recognized the tomatoes, but could not identify the white balls or green slices.

"I'd offer you wine, but I suspect it would put you to sleep."

She nodded, not because she remembered having

anything called wine, but because it was easier to agree with him at the moment. Easier to keep from focusing on the yawning blank spaces in her memory.

"How about iced tea?"

"Fine."

"With sugar?"

"Fine," she answered again.

He filled two glasses with clear cubes, then reached into the refrigerator, took out a pitcher and poured amber liquid into each.

As she carried the glasses to the table, they felt cold in her hand, and she set them down quickly. When he pulled out a chair and sat so did she. He looked at her, then took a sip of the tea. She did the same, feeling tension hum back and forth between them. Tension neither one of them was prepared to acknowledge.

Seeking some other focus of her attention, she studied the plate of what he had called fettuccine Alfredo. She could see him winding the white strands onto a fork. It seemed like a strange kind of procedure, and it was a challenge to work neatly as she imitated the process, conscious that he was watching her. Quickly she lifted the utensil to her mouth and slurped. A burst of flavor made her gasp.

He stirred his fork in his bowl. "You don't like it?"

"It…it is wonderful," she managed, after she had chewed and swallowed, loving the contrast of the slightly firm strands with the rich, creamy sauce. Eagerly, she took another bite. Then another.

He was watching her. "You look like you're starving."

"This is so good."

"What kind of cuisine would you say it is?" he asked.

"Does it matter?"

"You've never had Italian food?" he pressed, ignoring her previous assurance that she loved the dish.

"Pizza. Spaghetti," she answered, caught off balance.

He was staring at her oddly.

"Is English a foreign language for you?" he asked in what sounded like an abrupt change of topic.

She took another sip of the iced tea, wondering why anyone would deliberately make a drink cold. "I...do not—don't know."

"You don't remember?"

"What were you doing while I was getting dressed—thinking up questions to ask me?"

"I was cooking dinner."

"And thinking of questions. Is that your interrogation technique? Feed the prisoner, then pounce when you have her off guard?"

He leaned back in his seat. "I wouldn't call it an interrogation."

"What would you call it?"

"Maybe trying to understand why you tossed me in the water."

She looked down, twisting her fork in the food. This time, when she ate more of the fettuccine, she barely tasted it.

He was watching her consideringly. Finally he said, "I guess you don't know if you can trust me. And I've got the same problem with you."

"Yes," she whispered, wondering if she had spoken loudly enough for him to hear her.

"There's something...bad going on in Hermosa Harbor," he said. "You could be mixed up in it. If you tell me how you're involved, I could help you."

She fiddled with the glass, running her fingers over the condensation on the smooth sides.

"Okay, I understand you're scared." He leaned back in his chair and crossed his legs at the ankles. "But I've figured out some things about you already. You don't seem to know a lot about the culture. There are big blanks in your general knowledge. That could mean you've entered the country as an illegal alien. But you don't seem to know much about yourself, either. Which makes me wonder if you have a memory problem. If so, I would imagine that would be terrifying."

"Thank you, Dr. Freud," she answered, wondering where the reference had come from.

He laughed. "Nice recovery. But you've got a ways to go."

When she pressed her lips together, he said, "I'm good at getting people out of trouble."

"Why?" she demanded, because it felt so tempting to accept his offer. But she knew deep down that she could easily jump the wrong way.

He gave her a little smile. "Well, I've got enough money to live comfortably. But an idle life can be kind of boring. So I spice it up by doing favors for friends."

She thought the answer was evasive—as evasive as she had been in *her* answers to *his* questions.

"I do not know much about you," she pressed.

"I'm a pretty ordinary guy."

"I do not think so. I think you are trained in…survival skills…combat…and interrogation."

"Oh, yeah?"

"Where did you get the scar on your chin?" she pressed.

He laughed. "That's hardly spymaster material. I was six years old, and my mom had bought a watermelon.

She said it was for a picnic, but I wanted some right then. So I pushed a chair across the kitchen, got a knife out of the drawer and tried to cut into the rind. But the knife wouldn't go in. It bounced up and got me in the chin. I guess I'm lucky I didn't do more damage."

"Oh." Captivated by the story, she tried to picture the determined little boy. She knew it was not polite to ask about a person's history, but she found herself saying, "Tell me some more about yourself."

"Like what?"

"Where did you grow up?"

"Chicago."

A city in the middle of the United States. She was afraid he would stop there, but he went on.

"My dad was a chemist with a drug company. My mom worked part-time in a library. We had a real *Leave It to Beaver* household."

He might have been speaking a foreign language, but she hung on the words, then fought to keep him talking when he stopped abruptly.

"They are still in Chicago?"

"They were both killed in a car wreck."

"I am so sorry," she said even as a picture formed in her mind of a little girl being wrenched out of a woman's arms. She had to clamp her lip between her teeth to hold back the sound that tried to rise in her throat.

"It was a few years ago," he said, pulling her attention back to him.

"Tell me some more things," she said quickly.

His eyes had taken on a faraway look. "I was a Boy Scout. I loved camping trips best. When my troop went to the Grand Canyon, I wanted to take a raft ride down the Colorado, but I never did it. Of course, after I moved East, I tried some of the rapids back here.''

She was not sure what to ask next, but she wanted to know more. School. He would have gone to school. ''What was your favorite subject in school?'' she asked.

He laughed again. ''Football.''

She had thought that was a game. ''Oh. Where did you learn to cook?''

''My mom thought my brother and I should be able to take care of ourselves. I can sew on buttons, too.''

She leaned forward. ''How did you end up here?''

''After college I took a government job. It was exciting for a while. Then I kind of burned out.''

''You were burned?''

He smiled and shook his head. ''Let's get back to you. You're no ordinary woman in trouble.''

She swallowed her disappointment that he wanted to stop talking about himself. She craved more, much more. But he had switched his attention to her.

''You're a trained fighter,'' he said.

''Am I?''

''Don't be modest.''

''You think that is good?''

''Depending on who trained you.''

''What do you mean?''

''The good guys or the bad guys.''

''Give me a score card,'' she demanded, pulling a phrase from somewhere in her brain.

''I was hoping you could do that.''

She was considering the statement when he raised his head and turned slowly toward the window. ''Damn,'' he muttered.

''What is wrong?''

''There's someone watching us.''

"Watching us? How?"

"With Knockers?"

"An interesting name for them."

"With binoculars. It's that bastard Hap Henderson."

When she turned her head and started to twist around, Max stopped her.

"Don't let him know I've spotted him."

She faced forward again, trying to keep her shoulders from going rigid. "Who is he?"

"He lives in the marina. He's been keeping an eye on me."

"Why?"

"I guess it's his job to check out strangers."

"Strangers?"

"I've only been in town a month. The point is, when he came snooping around here a little earlier, I told him I had a heavy date with you. I think we'd better make sure he believes I was telling the truth."

"How?" she asked, hearing the breathy quality of her voice.

"I think you'll catch on." He pushed back his chair and stood up, then rounded the table, reached down and gently pulled her to her feet.

"All you have to do is convince Henderson that you're enjoying yourself in my company." As he spoke, he eased her into his arms. "Which means, you should start by not pushing me away," he said as she automatically raised her hands and flattened them against his chest.

"Relax," he growled, his mouth hovering only inches from hers.

Impossible. When his lips touched hers, she struggled to control the panic that bloomed inside her.

But panic was swamped almost at once by a host of

other sensations. The feel of his mouth on hers. The rich male scent of his body. The strong bands of his arms, enfolding her.

Somewhere in the back of her mind, she knew she should be frightened of him. At the very least, she should protect her honor. But those thoughts were driven deeper into the background as he moved his lips against hers.

It was a tender exploration, almost questing, and she had the feeling that if she protested, he would stop.

But she knew if she did, she would be the loser. Just as it was impossible to admit her weakness on a conscious level, it was also impossible to deny that she liked the place where he'd put her. In his arms.

This had not been her choice. Perhaps that was what made it all right to enjoy the way his mouth coaxed a response from hers and the way her body absorbed the heat from his and gave the warmth back to him.

She had closed her eyes in order to block out everything except Max Dakota. Leaning into him, she felt a small sound rise in her throat. A needy sound that surprised her perhaps as much as it seemed to surprise him.

"That's right," he murmured, as his lips continued to move against hers.

One of his large hands played with her hair, combing through the strands. The other flattened itself against her back, stroking her and stoking the unaccustomed sensations she felt building inside her.

He made a growling noise deep in his chest as he slipped his hand under the hem of the shirt and slid it upward, splaying it against the bare skin of her back.

Had she ever felt anything as exquisite as his fingers against her bare skin?

His touch was light, but it seemed to blaze a trail of fire along her nerve endings.

She had forgotten why he had taken her in his arms. Forgotten everything but his taste, his touch. And her own out-of-kilter response.

Her breasts ached, especially the nipples. They had contracted painfully, and the only way she could ease the tight sensation was to press them against his chest.

That was no help. It only made her crave more and more—of something, she could not say what it was.

But suddenly she needed to get as close to him as possible. If she had ever felt this desperation, she could not remember when. Surely if she remembered anything from before he had pulled her from the water, it should be this. This man-woman flare of heat.

All she could do was lean into him, caught by the steamy pleasure of the contact.

"Annie," he said against her mouth, nibbling with his lips and then his teeth.

She liked the way he said the name with an edge of desperation. He had given her that name, which made it all the better.

Still, part of her was standing back, watching the two of them together in dumb fascination.

He was sweeping her along with him to some dark, dangerous place she had never been. At least, she could not imagine that she had ever felt this way before. This reckless. This out of control. This good.

Between them she felt a hard ridge pressing against her middle. She wanted to move against it, and when she did, he made low sounds of approval.

His hand swept over her ribs, and she remembered something she had totally forgotten.

The tattoo.

She did not know what it was, but she knew it was vital that Max not find it.

"Stop." As she issued the command, she pushed on his shoulder.

His eyes blinked open, and he stared down at her, his face as full of confusion as she knew hers must be.

She had pushed him away because she knew it was what she must do. Not because it was what she wanted.

To him, to herself, she uttered an apology. "I am sorry."

His hands dropped to his sides, and she saw his fists clench and unclench. "No problem," he muttered. "I was only thinking we'd convince Hap you were my girlfriend. But that went totally over the edge."

"Edge of what?" she asked, hearing the breathless quality of her voice.

He laughed, the sound rough and deep. "You have a strange way with words."

"Do I?"

"Oh, yeah." Turning away from her, he ran his hand through his hair.

He stood with his back to her, his shoulders and arms shouting out his tension.

She pressed her own palms to her thighs. She ached to go to him so he could fold her back into his arms. But she stayed where she was, because caution had been drummed into her.

By whom?

She did not remember. All she knew was that she had violated some important rule. And she did not even know what it was.

Chapter Five

The emotions warring in Annie made her want to run. But she couldn't think where to go, so she stayed where she was, her feet rooted to the floor.

Max snatched up his plate and carried it back to the galley.

She watched what he did, then did the same with her own plate and then with the salad bowl.

She had just set down the bowl on the galley counter when the sound of a buzzer made her jump. *Carp!* She was reacting again to a loud noise. Why? She had no answer. No answer! And that was only a small part of the nightmare she was facing. The black void in her brain.

The look on her face must have prompted his response. "That's the phone. It's got a strange ringer," he said, crossing to the kitchen and reaching for an instrument hanging on the wall. She watched him press a button, then carry the receiver to her ear. She knew about phones, but hadn't expected one to sound like that.

"Hello?"

He listened for several moments, a number of different emotions registering on his face. Annoyance. Guilt. She wasn't sure what else.

"My plans have changed," he said.

She had no business listening to the conversation or watching him so closely. In fact, she shouldn't even be interested. But step by step, she moved closer.

As Max watched her walk toward him, his posture stiffened. She went still, but she was close enough to hear the sound of a woman's loud voice through the speaker.

"I was expecting you this evening," the woman said with a note of accusation.

"I'm sorry," Max answered. "Something came up."

"Hap said you have company."

"What is he—my keeper?"

"He just mentioned that he thought you wouldn't be coming to the club this evening."

He glanced at Annie, then away. "Right. My girlfriend from up north is here."

"If you have a girlfriend, why were you hanging around with me?" the voice from the receiver demanded.

Max glanced at Annie again, then hunched his shoulders and turned partially away. "Nicki, I'm sorry. She and I..." He stopped and started again. "The way we left things, I wasn't sure we were getting back together."

The words and the casual way he spoke them made Annie's stomach knot. She knew he wasn't telling the truth. She knew she wasn't his girlfriend from up north or anywhere else.

She stopped herself. Well, she supposed that by some wild convergence of events, it *could* be true. Anything could be true, since she couldn't remember anyone from her past.

But what he was saying felt wrong. Which meant he was lying, both in what he said and the way he said it. He was lying to protect her, she told herself. Somehow that didn't help.

"I wouldn't put it that way," Max was saying, and she realized she'd missed Nicki's response.

In the next second, there was a loud click on the other end of the line. Max replaced the phone and turned back to her.

"Who was that?" she asked, again aware that the answer was none of her business.

He watched her closely as he said, "Nicki Armstrong. She owns a nightclub in town, Nicki's Paradise."

Annie ignored the explanation and went right to the personal relationship. "And you are…having sexual relations with her when you are not fixing me dinner?" she heard herself say, then felt her cheeks flush because the topic was so wildly inappropriate.

He tipped his head to one side. "Sexual relations. That's kind of a stuffy way to put it, don't you think?"

She shrugged, then said, "I should not have asked about your liaison with her. It was none of my business."

Max spoke slowly and decisively. "I don't mind answering the question. I was friendly with her. I know she wanted it to go further than that. But I didn't think I should."

"Why not?"

She saw him shift his weight from one foot to the other. "Because I didn't have the right feelings for her. And I'm not into casual sex."

"Oh." She wanted to ask him what he felt for *her*. When he had kissed her a few moments ago, it had not felt anything like casual. He was probably planning to do a lot more, until she'd stopped him. But he'd turned her loose the moment she'd protested.

"So, is Nicki a friend of yours?" he suddenly asked. The question threw her completely off balance.

"No," she answered automatically.

"You don't know her?"

"If I do, I don't remember," she answered, remembering to use the contraction.

"You're sticking with the amnesia alibi I helped you concoct?"

"It isn't an alibi. It's the truth! Why is it impossible for you to believe me?"

"Because your loss of memory is so convenient."

"If you say so."

His face softened. "Maybe whatever happened to you was so traumatic that you can't deal with it."

"Or maybe I have no choice," she answered immediately. His explanation implied she was weak. No matter her identity, she knew that wasn't true.

Though she wanted to drop the subject, she thought back over some of the things he had said previously. Almost against her will, she found herself asking, "If I did know her, what illegal activity would we be engaged in together—in your considered opinion?"

"I was hoping you'd tell me."

She raised her arm in an exasperated gesture, then let it fall to her side. "I can't."

"Or won't."

"Can't," she corrected, suddenly feeling as if she was trying to breathe around a giant obstruction in her windpipe. She had to get away from him. She had to start thinking straight. "I'm too tired to keep going back and forth with you. Maybe we should leave it until tomorrow."

"Okay," he answered. "Maybe you'll have a new outlook in the morning."

"You mean, maybe I will stop lying to you?" she asked, unable to keep her fragile emotions out of her voice.

"You said it, not me."

She clenched her teeth, then deliberately relaxed her jaw. "You have somewhere for me to sleep—besides your bed?"

"Yes." He turned on his heel and started for the stairs.

She followed him below.

"You can have this cabin," he said, opening another door across from the head. It led to a sleeping chamber that was much smaller than the one where he'd taken her earlier. Instead of one large bed, there were two bunks against the wall.

"It's small, but it's comfortable," he said, flipping a wall switch that turned on several recessed ceiling lights. "I'll leave an extra toothbrush and T-shirt for you in the head. You can sleep in the shirt if you want."

"Thank you," she murmured, fighting the impulse to give in and trust him. She wanted his help, but at the same time, she couldn't succumb to that weakness. And she didn't even know if he was lying about a spy in the marina. Maybe he'd just used that as a way to trick her into his arms.

Trying not to let anything in her mind show on her face, she closed the door. Alone, she leaned back against the solid barrier for several moments, letting her heart rate slow. When she was feeling more in control, she opened her eyes again and scanned the room.

MAX WENT BACK upstairs to the lounge and began to wash the dishes. Neither he nor his guest had eaten much of the food, which wasn't surprising. Hap hadn't given them much time for dinner.

Yeah, right. Hap.

He was the reason Nicki had called. Max had heard the edge of anger in her voice the moment he'd answered the phone. But he couldn't blame Nicki and Hap for what had happened between the meal and the phone call.

He'd announced that someone had been spying on them. So that meant they had to put on a good show?

"Give me a break, Dakota," he muttered. He could have simply slung his arm around her and nuzzled her neck. There had been no earthly reason he had sought her lips with his—except that he'd been thinking about it since he'd first set her on his bed. He'd wanted to do it. So he'd seized the excuse. And if she hadn't been the one to call things to a halt, they would have been naked when Nicki called.

He bit out a curse, thinking that the higher levels of his brain had stopped functioning a while ago and he'd better get them back into full service—before he blew this assignment.

His hands mechanically washed the dishes as he considered his behavior. And how he was going to alter it.

Too bad Annie reminded him of Steph. Not that she looked like her, of course. Her hair color and features were different, although her body type was similar. But it wasn't physical details that made him think of his dead wife. It was the way she behaved. She was stuck in deep muck, and she was doing her best to wade out of it by herself. Her memory was shot to hell, or she was pretending it was. Either way, she was determined not to cave in or go to pieces.

No, she was willing to take risks that might be unacceptable. His fingers clenched on the fork he was washing, and he deliberately eased up on the pressure.

Her stubborn bravery was making him want to help her. But that wasn't the reason he was in Hermosa Harbor. He had a job to do. He was investigating a murder, and he had a woman on his boat he couldn't trust. He'd better remember both those facts.

So had she been playacting during the kiss? He might be out of practice, but he still believed he could tell the real thing. Annie had responded to him. He'd felt the heat coming off her, felt the way she'd gone all boneless and pliant in his arms. Heard her indrawn breath when he'd splayed his hands against her silky skin.

Just thinking about it had made him hard again. Cursing, he rinsed the cutlery and clattered it into the dish drainer, then spilled the soapy water from the dishpan into the sink and turned to stare out into the darkness of the marina. Her response to the kiss was beside the point. And he'd better keep that in mind. He'd also best remember that no matter what inappropriate emotions he felt for this woman, she could be dangerous.

CHARLES RELAXED on the motel-room bed with the remote, flipping through the channels on the television. All he could find was crap, but what had he expected, here in the middle of Florida vacation land? Hell, anywhere in the good old U.S. of A., for that matter. The society was a mess. The culture was a mess. The government was a mess. But he planned to fix all that.

Setting down the remote, he picked up the dessert he'd brought home from his restaurant dinner. Apple pie. The first bite told him it was the kind he liked, with slightly tart fruit and a flaky crust. He began to eat, thinking that he was getting close to his last meal. But he was ready for that. It was one of the conditions he'd accepted.

He fluffed up the pillows and lay back on the bed without bothering to take off his shoes. He had paid for the motel room with a credit card—with the new name he had been using since last week. Actually, he had changed his name many times in the past few years. He had a new identity now. Even a new face. Once he had been a guest of the U.S. government, and they had taken his picture—from the front and from the side. Well, the face they had photographed didn't exist anymore. Even his fingerprints had been planed off. The new identity was courtesy of some friends who were willing to finance his project. They had their reasons. He had let them think his were the same. But he had his own agenda.

While he ate the pie, he got out a map of the kill zone and began to study it. Really, he'd already memorized the details. But it never hurt to take extra precautions—especially when you were planning to take terrorism to a new level.

THE SUIT ANNIE had worn was still in the head. She took it back to her room, along with the salve Max had given her. After smoothing more of the cream on her chest, she rolled up the near-dry suit and stuffed it in a corner in a bag. Then she turned in a circle, giving herself a full view of the room.

It was small but nice. Cozy. When she pressed on the mattress, it felt thick and springy.

She had said she was tired. But that wasn't the reason she wanted to go off by herself. She needed to get away from the intensity of Max's gaze. Well, not just his gaze. From the intensity of the man. And the feelings he called forth from some deep, hidden part of her.

Lifting her hand, she pressed it against her lips, lightly rubbing her sensitive skin, caught by the memory of the heat and pressure of his mouth on hers.

The kiss had felt wonderful. Like the pressure of his hands against her skin. She closed her eyes, unable to stop the remembered sensations from washing over her. She had wanted more. She still wanted more.

Yet, she had made him stop. She remembered why she had pushed him away. Snatching her hand from her lips, she reached under her shirt and found the place she'd been afraid he'd touch. The tattoo. The scared, vulnerable part of her had wanted the mark to be a figment of her imagination. But it was still there. She could feel it.

She pressed her fingers hard against it and felt a small burst of pain. The sensation was enough to bring her mind back to where it should be.

She had to figure out who she was. Where she was. Why she was in this particular place of all places on earth. Because she felt the pressure of some monumental disaster constricting her chest, making it almost impossible to breathe.

Deliberately, she dragged in a lungful of air, then let it out slowly as she took stock of the little room. There were two portholes in the far wall, but she was pretty sure they were too small for her to climb through.

The door was the only way out. It wasn't her preference, but there was nothing she could do about it. She moved to the small desk against the wall and began opening drawers. In the middle one, she found a pad of paper and a ballpoint pen, which she set on the desktop.

Then she poked through some of the other drawers. She found a woman's yellow bathing-suit top, a navy-blue sock made out of some silky material and a box with a picture of a man and a woman embracing on the front. The way she and Max had been embracing. Close and intimate. Inside were half-a-dozen foil packets.

Condoms. And she knew what they were used for, too. Sexual intercourse.

Because she'd used them with a man? In her mind, she tried to take the heated scene with Max further. But she couldn't do it—at least not from any personal experience she remembered.

Putting the box back, she dug for more buried treasure and found a stiff piece of paper with a picture of a sailboat. Below it was a calendar. As she looked at the year, her throat tightened. She didn't know whether the calendar was current or if it had been shoved into the drawer because it was out-of-date.

A shiver went through her.

She was so out of touch that she didn't even know the year. That was bad enough, yet something else teased at the edge of her mind—something she should know.

Something so frightening that it threatened to choke off her breath again.

Going back to the drawers, she dragged out a stack of shiny pieces of paper held together at the folded edge with two small metal strips. On the front was the picture of a grim looking white-haired man. Above him was the word *Newsweek* in white letters on a red background strip.

Her fingers clenched on the paper. *Newsweek.* A magazine with the week's events. Her heart was pounding as she searched the cover for a date and found it under the title. It was for April 20. In the year after the calendar.

That meant she still had time. The thought flickered in her head, but she didn't know what it meant. Time for what?

And as with the calendar, she didn't even know how long the magazine had been in the drawer. Maybe her time was already up.

She unclenched her fingers from around the paper, then began to page through the magazine. She saw a map. A tall building. A man talking on the telephone.

On the next page was a dog leaping in the air to catch a flat circle in its mouth. A Frisbee. She knew the word. But except on a computer screen, she was sure that she had never seen one. Or a dog, for that matter.

The colored pictures made her head swim. She'd been uncertain of herself earlier. Looking at the photographs made her feel as if she'd dropped into the water from an alien spaceship.

Quickly she flipped the page again and found herself staring down at another photograph, of a building reduced to rubble. Sitting in front of it was a little girl clutching a rag doll.

A sound rose in her throat. A sound of grief impossible to hold back.

Details came at her like a bombardment of stones. The child had blond hair and blue eyes. She looked about five years old. Her face and clothing were dirty, and she was clutching the doll as though it was her only friend in the world.

For a moment Annie was that child, lost and alone. Everything safe and familiar had been ripped away, and she was adrift in the rubble of her young life.

The picture blurred, and she knew she was crying. She was sure she hadn't cried in a long time. But now tears welled in her eyes and flowed freely down her cheeks.

She stretched out her hand toward the picture, aching to comfort the child. She felt the need with an all-consuming desperation.

She had to help her, and she had to help herself, too. If she knew anything in the world, she knew that much.

Gently she closed the magazine and laid it back in the drawer, which she carefully shut. Then she picked up the pen she had left on the desk and began drawing something.

When she finished, she stared at what she had done. It looked like the same symbol she had found tattooed under her arm. She had no idea what it meant. She only knew she had to wrap the sheet of paper in plastic and put it in a certain place in a certain building. Someplace in the downtown area. An image of the structure came to her. She didn't know where it was but she knew she had to find it.

But not now. Not yet. Not until Max was out of the way. With a sigh she eased onto the bottom bunk, then lay there tensely listening for him and listening to the sound of the water slapping against the sides of the boat.

MAX WAITED on the main deck until he had heard no sounds from Annie's cabin for half an hour. Then he carefully transferred the fingerprints from the glass she had used to a special piece of tape, which he took down to his room and scanned into a computer file. He sent the image off to Randolph Security over the encrypted computer line. They handled a lot of background details for the Light Street Detective Agency, and he knew that through them, he could tap into the FBI fingerprint database.

Hunter Kelley, who was on duty that evening, received the message and accessed the government criminal-identification system.

While Max waited for Annie's prints to be compared to the millions on file, he stopped in the head and looked for the suit she'd been wearing. But she'd taken it away, and he wasn't going to barge into her cabin to find it.

The conversation with her at dinner had made him think about himself, about how he had gotten here. He'd been an idealistic kid. Idealistic enough to believe he could make a difference in the struggle of good—meaning the United States—against the bad guys, like the terrorists who wanted to wreck the American way of life. He was more cynical now. Harder. He'd lost many of his illusions in the first few years as a spook. The rest of them had died with Steph.

He wasn't really surprised fifteen minutes later, when Hunter's message told him there was no match in the database.

Presumably, then, the woman he called Annie Oakley was not a known criminal. And she hadn't worked at a job requiring her to be fingerprinted.

"You have a lead on the Jacobson murder?" Hunter asked in a secure instant message.

Max hesitated for a moment before typing a reply. "No lead. Just a suspicious individual," he answered, knowing he was being evasive with a colleague who trusted him.

"Keep us posted."

"Will do." He pushed away from the desk. Damn. He was in a very sticky situation. What if Annie's interests were different from Light Street's interests? Which way would he jump?

Merely considering the question shocked him. He knew what the answer had to be. He was being paid to do a job. More than that, the Light Street group in Baltimore had thrown him a lifeline when he'd been drowning.

All of that was true. So why wasn't he sure he would do the right thing?

Chapter Six

Priorities.

Max sighed. In the end, he knew his priorities.

Meanwhile he'd have to persuade Annie that it was to her advantage to let Uncle Max help her get out of trouble. Uncle Max! Who was he kidding? That wasn't the relationship he wanted with her.

Would he find anything more on her in law-enforcement databases? Though he hoped not, he felt duty bound to try. After signing off with Light Street, he tapped into the Florida State Troopers hot line. There was no missing-persons report that matched his visitor's description. He extended the search to Georgia, then other East Coast states. He even checked in with the California system, each time reinforcing his conviction that as far as the police were concerned, she didn't exist.

He'd bet that she wasn't born in the U.S. and that she hadn't been here long. But she was missing from *somewhere*. Either nobody knew she was gone, they didn't care or they assumed she had died when she'd gone into the water.

He sat for several minutes contemplating that last cheery thought. Then he turned off the computer, stood up and stretched cramped muscles. After slipping off his shoes and socks, he padded down the hall and listened at the door to the smaller cabin. He heard nothing, and he was tempted to open the door and see if she was asleep. What would she be wearing? He had no trouble picturing her naked. Not after seeing her in that second-skin suit. He clenched his jaw, then turned and went into the head. After using the facilities and brushing his teeth, he made his way back to his room, thinking that he'd better get some sleep. He had the feeling he was going to need it.

He shucked off his pants and Hawaiian shirt, then climbed into bed in his briefs and closed his eyes.

For a while he dozed, then he was back in the nightmare that had taken over his life in San Marcos. He hadn't dreamed about Stephanie in a long time. Now, once again, he was in the mountains of a Latin American country, hiding in the darkness of a cave.

As they had so many times, he and Stephanie were arguing about the assignment. He couldn't see her face, because it was too dangerous to switch on a light. But he could hear the steel in her voice.

Six years earlier, they had been in basic training in the Peregrine Connection together. They had been drawn to each other, and both had been happy about getting their dual assignments.

He had liked the way her philosophy matched his— live for the moment. That had been one of the things that made her a wonderful lover. In bed, her total concentration was on the pleasure they gave each other. And on leave, she threw herself into adventures like white-water rafting and hang gliding with the enthusiasm of a kid.

When they'd gotten married, he wanted more. He wanted to settle down and start a family. But every time he brought it up, she'd tell him they'd do it after one more mission—then one more.

So they'd ended up tracking rebels in San Marcos and in deep trouble, because a chance encounter with the wrong troop had gotten their radio destroyed, and she wanted to go down into the village where the rebels were hiding to use their communications equipment.

"It's too dangerous. We need to get out of here."

"Are you chicken?" she asked, tossing the question at him as though he were a raw recruit.

"No, I'm a realist. We already got creamed by the bad guys. We can't take on a whole squad of them by ourselves."

"I think we can. And if you don't want to help me, I'll do it by myself."

He had no choice. He couldn't let her go alone. So he went with her down the trail. The rebels were waiting for them about a quarter mile from the village. Suddenly they were in the middle of a hail of bullets.

Stephanie's scream echoed in his ears, getting louder...shriller...

Until Max sat bolt upright in bed, mercifully ending the sound. But not the reality.

His wife was dead and somehow he'd survived. Somehow he'd crawled away into the bushes and made it to the river with a bullet in his leg. From there he'd let the current take him downstream, into safe territory. But into the heartache that had become life without Stephanie.

A SMILE FLICKERED on Nicki Armstrong's face as she surveyed her domain from a private table in the corner of the nightclub.

It was after midnight, but red, blue and yellow lights

alternated across the ceiling, casting their beams on about fifty men and women—mostly young and well dressed—enjoying the jumping atmosphere of Nicki's Paradise. Some were out on the dance floor gyrating to the pulsing disco beat, the standard weeknight music option. Others were at the bar or the small tables ringing the wooden dance floor.

In about an hour, the crowd would start to thin. But now the club was still full of revelers, because anyone who wanted to have a good time in Hermosa Harbor knew that Nicki's Paradise was the place to be.

It wasn't the part of her business empire that brought in the most money. But it was certainly the most fun. She liked being the queen of her own realm, and she liked keeping her finger on every aspect of the operation—from the kinds of liquor she stocked to the kind of handgun her bartender kept out of sight under the counter and the size of the payoff she handed the local cops every two weeks.

Above the sound of the music, a noise at the other side of the room snagged her attention. Two young men were spoiling for a fight.

From the corner of her eye, she saw the tall, muscular bouncer amble across the dance floor toward them. When Paul reached them, his tree-trunk arms hanging easily at his sides, he asked if there was a problem, or words to that effect. Over the sound of the dance music, she couldn't hear what her bouncer was saying. But she knew that Paul would take care of the problem.

Her attention switched again as she saw Hap Henderson step through the silvery curtain at the entrance and look around before weaving his way through the tables to the bar. Dave, who was on duty, glanced in her direction. When she nodded, he fixed Hap his usual planter's punch. Too bad the man had expensive taste in rum. He insisted on a brand from the Cayman Islands that cost the earth.

Turning, Hap leaned against the bar and sipped his drink, watching her across the crowded room with a speculative gaze. He'd already spoken to her on the phone and told her about Max's visitor. Now she wondered what else he was planning to spring on her. As he watched, she swept her long, red hair back over her shoulder and recrossed her legs, secure in the knowledge that her thighs were tanned and firm, taunting Hap with what he couldn't have.

Two years ago, after she'd made it clear she wasn't interested in warming his bed, he'd started getting his jollies by needling her. She would have gotten rid of him months ago, but he'd had the bucks to finance some very profitable deals. So she was stuck with him as a business partner—unless she wanted to take drastic measures. She figured it was better not to press her luck.

Hap left the bar and sidled over to her table. Without waiting for an invitation, he pulled out one of the curved-back chrome chairs and sat down.

"So," he said, pitching his voice above the music and the background chatter, "what do you think about Max?"

She gave him a sharp look, and he pressed his lips together.

Didn't he have enough sense to keep his mouth shut until they had some privacy? Probably nobody was listening, but you could never be sure.

For several minutes, as she avoided further conversation, she pretended to be fascinated by the dancers out on the floor. A good-looking guy caught her eye and smiled. She smiled back, thinking that if Max Dakota didn't want to make love with her, there were plenty of other candidates.

Then a prickly sensation at the back of her neck made her twist in her seat and look back toward the hallway that led to the rest rooms, the phones and the office. In the shadows she saw the figure of a large, broad-shouldered man and knew her other business partner had arrived. He stayed out of the light, as well he should, because there were people here who would be inhibited by his presence.

"Our friend is here," she said in a barely audible voice, then pushed back her chair and headed for the hallway.

Hap was a few steps behind her as she opened the door to the office and entered. Sheriff Bert Trainer was already there, taking up most of the floor space and the oxygen in the room.

Trainer made her nervous. But then, he made everybody nervous. He was an odd guy. Intimidation was his main mode of operation, and it was a very effective tool in keeping the undesirable element in Hermosa Harbor in line.

His beefy face looked as if he had a perpetual sunburn. His eyelids drooped over watery blue eyes, and his expression might have been described as slack, until his steel jaws snapped together and his lids lifted in sudden interest, transforming him from a sleepy cop to a spider ready to pounce on his prey.

It was lucky they had come to an accommodation when she'd first arrived in town, Nicki thought as she sat down behind her walnut desk and gave him an easy nod. As long as he got his cut, he didn't give her any trouble.

Still, she had to remind herself not to swivel back

and forth nervously in her contour chair as the two men took the guest chairs across from her.

Trainer got right to business, fixing Hap with a speculative gaze. "So why did you call this meeting?" he said.

"There's a new development at the marina," the other man answered.

Trainer tipped his head to the side. "Oh, yeah?"

"Max Dakota is entertaining a young lady."

The sheriff looked from the informant to Nicki. "Sorry, I can't arrest him for that."

"I wasn't suggesting it," she snapped.

"I've got some pictures." Hap reached into his pocket and took out several color photographs. Although she wanted to pretend disinterest, Nicki found herself leaning forward to get a better look. The photos weren't sharp, nor were they from a good angle. Obviously, Hap had taken them with a telephoto lens through the window of *The Wrong Stuff*.

One showed the marina resident sitting across the table from a slender blonde wearing a baggy aloha shirt and shorts. The next one showed the two of them standing beside the table in a close clinch, their lips fused. The third showed the same scene, only Max's hand was under the woman's shirt.

"He told me she was his girlfriend from up north," Nicki said.

"You think that's the God's honest truth?" Trainer asked.

"It could be. But the thing is, nobody saw her arrive at the marina," Hap said. "Just all of a sudden, she was there. Makes me wonder if somehow he picked her up while he was supposed to be out fishing."

"What would be the point of that?" Nicki asked.

Hap shrugged. "Alls I'm telling you is that I found him entertaining a lady friend. But she didn't drive herself there. And she didn't ride up in a cab, and she didn't come in a boat that docked at the marina."

Trainer looked thoughtful.

"I couldn't get a good look at her. The question is, could she be that chick who was nosing around here a few months ago? I mean, it looks like they're the same body type. The same hair. The same ass—"

The sheriff's voice interrupted Hap's recitations. "You don't have to worry about the woman who was here a few months ago."

"Because?"

"Because I had a very frank chat with her, encouraging her to leave town. I don't think she'll be coming back to Hermosa Harbor."

Because she's dead, Nicki surmised. That was what Trainer had implied. Or was that a ploy? Was he lying through his teeth? Was there really something going on between him and Max's friend that he didn't want her or Hap to know about?

She didn't voice the questions because playing it safe with Bert Trainer was always the best policy. She respected his opinions, gave him his cut most importantly, and, had let him know that the damaging information she had on him would be sent right to the *Miami Herald* and a New York law firm if anything unexpected happened to her.

"I'll keep an eye on the situation," Hap said.

"And I'll stop by the marina later," Trainer added, letting the sentence hang in the air.

For what? Nicki wondered. To make the woman wish she'd never come to Hermosa Harbor? Or to confer with her?

Nicki was going to have to figure it out soon, because there was a shipment coming in any day. Nothing was going to interfere with its sale and distribution. So if Max Dakota and his friend were planning something, too bad for them.

"Keep me posted," Nicki said. Then she stood. As far as she was concerned, the meeting was over.

SOMETHING WOKE MAX from the light sleep he'd finally fallen into an hour earlier. He'd been ready for trouble ever since he pulled Annie out of the water, and he was instantly alert. The Glock that had been under his pillow was now in his hand.

His eyes and ears strained in the darkness, and he heard a low, moaning sound coming from down the hall. From Annie's room. He uttered a silent curse. Had the people who had pushed her off the bridge found her—with Hap's help?

Quickly he crossed to the door, opened it noiselessly, then started down the hall, the Glock at the ready.

He reached her door and slid it open, then stood with the gun in a two-handed grip, ready to mow the bastards down.

His gaze darted swiftly around the small cabin, then zeroed in on the bottom bunk where Annie lay, wearing the T-shirt he'd given her that evening. She was alone, her head moving on the pillow, her eyes closed, her voice high and keening. Apparently he wasn't the only one having nightmares tonight.

He wanted to go to her, wake her from the bad dream and comfort her. Yet at the same time, he was pretty sure he could learn something from what he was seeing and hearing.

"Please," she moaned. "Why…want me?"

Crossing to the bunk, he set the gun down on the floor where she couldn't see it.

Her words were low and strung together, and he had to bend toward her to hear them. Even so, he wasn't sure he was getting everything she was saying.

Someone must have answered her, because she shook her head violently. "Please...no. Don't ask that."

After a moment's pause, she said, "Never come back...?"

It sounded like a question, but he couldn't be sure.

Her face twisted, and she moaned. Beads of sweat stood out on her forehead, and he had to press his palm against his side to keep from wiping them away.

She was speaking again. "Don't hurt Suli... Please, no. Momma, help me!" The plea ended in a high, inarticulate sound.

Then there were no more words he could catch, only screams and moans as she writhed on the bed.

God, it sounded as if she was being tortured. Of course he couldn't be sure if the dream was the reliving of a real event or just a collection of horrors conjured up from the depths of her imagination.

But whatever was digging its razor-sharp claws into her, he couldn't take it for another millisecond. "Annie, wake up. You're all right. It's Max Dakota. You're safe with me."

He put his hands on her shoulders. Instantly she came up off the bed, fighting him, and he knew he had made an error in judgment. She might still be sleeping, but that made her no less dangerous.

At that moment, the need to keep her from killing him superseded all else.

"Annie, wake up!" he shouted as he wrapped his arms around her, coming down heavily on top of her in purely defensive mode as he kept talking, telling her who he was over and over again while she struggled under him, trying to kick him, bite him, inflict damage any way she could.

But he had the advantage of size and strength. No woman, no matter how well trained, was going to beat him in an endurance contest.

Well, that was what he thought. A few minutes—or was it hours?—later, he wasn't so sure who was going to win the life-or-death wrestling match.

They were both breathing hard, and he felt his own muscles trembling with the effort to keep her from damaging some important piece of his anatomy.

He was wondering if he could spring off her and put some distance between them when she went still. .

"You're awake," he breathed. "Thank God."

He'd turned his head away to protect his face from her teeth and was rewarded with a painful chomp on his earlobe. Cautiously, he turned back to her and saw her staring up at him with large, dazed eyes. She had never looked more beautiful, nor more vulnerable.

Before she could marshal her defenses, he shot a question at her. "Who is Suli?"

"My sister," she answered, surprising him with the information and the quick delivery.

He felt a surge of satisfaction. Finally they were getting somewhere. "Someone's holding her captive? Is that why you won't tell me what's going on? Is that the problem? If it is, I can help you."

A look of utter terror contorted her features. "I don't know!"

Instantly he wished he'd asked another question, something she could answer.

"But you remember her?" he pressed before he lost

any advantage he'd gained. As he watched, the terror and vulnerability he'd seen on her face vanished, and in their place was the iron resolve that both impressed and frustrated him.

She swallowed, and he thought she wasn't going to answer. But as he lay there with his heart pounding, she did speak—in a voice that was barely above a whisper. "She's little and weak. I promised Momma I would take care of her."

"She's younger than you?"

"Yes. And her genes are bad." She said the last part with a gulping sob.

"Why? What's wrong with her?"

She gave a helpless shrug, and he saw her grimace, making him realize he was still lying with his body pressed intimately to hers. He could feel her breasts, her hips, the tender place where her legs were splayed slightly.

"If I let you go, will you stop trying to kill me?" he asked, only half joking because he knew what she'd tried before.

"Yes."

Cautiously, still ready for a stealth attack, he shifted his body off her. She lay limply on the bunk, her breath ragged, her eyes closed.

They snapped open when he brushed the damp hair back from her face.

"Max," she murmured, "what are you doing here in bed with me?" She looked down the length of him. "You...you don't have any clothes on."

"I have on undershorts."

"Oh...well, then," she said, as though he'd told her he was dressed in a protective suit.

He didn't point out that in the light from the hallway,

he could see the dark circles of her nipples through the thin fabric of the T-shirt he'd lent her.

"You were having a bad dream."

She touched his bleeding ear and sucked in a sharp breath. "I hurt you. I'm so sorry."

"It's okay," he said, when really it stung like hell.

"You need to put something on it. A human bite can be dangerous."

"I'll take care of it in a minute. Right now I want you to tell me what you remember."

"Nothing."

"You remembered your sister."

"Yes. But that's all."

Was she lying? He couldn't be sure. "You were having a nightmare," he said. "Focus on that. See if you can remember what it was about."

She closed her eyes and was silent for a few moments. Then she said, "Angelo was yelling at me. He hit me."

"Why?"

"He was angry. He said I was the best one for the job. I had the most chance of success. I told him I could never do it."

Max reined in his own emotions as he kept the questions coming. "Who is Angelo? Your pimp? Your trainer? Your boss?"

She answered none of his questions. Not directly. "He's big. And he hurts you if you don't do what he says."

Max's hands closed over her shoulders. "Who is he?" he repeated.

She shrugged.

"You knew a few minutes ago!"

"Did I?" she asked, sounding as innocent as a child.

"You brought up his name."

"I know. But now…"

"Damn you! Stop playing games with me."

"I am not playing anything."

"Right," he sneered.

He felt a tiny tremor go through her. "Max, I swear I don't know. I do not know!" She almost screamed the words.

"Sure," he answered with similar frustration, then saw tears well up in her eyes. She was trying to hold them back, but they brimmed up and spilled over the edges. These first tears were like a crack in a dam. Seconds later, she was sobbing.

He caught her up in his arms, rocking her, stroking her back and hair.

She cried for a long time, hiding her face from him. Finally the sobs began to ease. He pulled a tissue from the box on the table beside the bunk and handed it to her.

"I'm sorry," she whispered after she blew her nose.

"For what?"

"I'm supposed to be strong."

"Who says?"

She gave an uncertain laugh. "I suppose that guy named Angelo. If I knew who he was, I'd tell you."

"Uh-huh."

"You don't believe me?"

"I want to believe you."

"Carp!"

She started to scoot toward the end of the bunk. He caught her wrist and pulled her back, and she came down against him, staring at him in the darkened room.

Her mouth was close to his. All he had to do was move a fraction of an inch and their lips would touch.

He knew he should move his head back. A bed was a dangerous place for the emotions he was feeling. Too much had happened in the past few hours for him to stay rational. Which was why he needed to be by himself. To think.

He should get up and leave the room before he got them both into serious trouble. Instead, he watched her eyes darken as he leaned closer.

She could have backed away. A moment ago she had tried to flee, and he had prevented her escape. Now he told himself he was giving her that option.

But she stayed stock-still, next to him in bed, waiting for whatever he was going to do. And he felt as if he'd suddenly been caught in a trap he'd created all on his own.

He could still stop, he told himself. Then she made a small sound deep in her throat, and he was utterly lost.

He answered with a greedy sigh and closed the gap between his lips and hers.

Lost in the taste of her, he forgot about the questions he'd been asking—and her hesitant answers. There was only the reality of the woman in his arms on this narrow bunk.

At first her body remained stiff. But as he kissed her, he felt her turn warm and pliant.

"Good. That's good," he murmured against her mouth.

"Oh, yes."

Her lips parted, and he took advantage of her surrender to slip his tongue inside for a deeper taste. He was instantly intoxicated with her essence; she tasted like spring flowers after a light rain.

But in truth, she filled every corner of his senses,

bringing feelings to life that he thought had died a year ago with Steph.

His heart was slamming against the inside of his chest as his arms came up to imprison her, only this time, there was no need to hold her in place. She moved closer to him, sliding her body along his until his erection was cradled in the cleft between her legs. Only two thin layers of fabric separated them—his briefs and the shorts she still wore.

He dragged in a shaky breath. So did she. He wanted more. He knew she did, too. But she had stopped him once, and he was afraid she would do it again.

He kept his mouth on hers, giving her deep, passionate kisses as he rolled to his side and fumbled with her T-shirt, dragging it up as far as he could without pulling it completely off.

He was trying to let her know that he wouldn't go too fast. But he was aware her breathing became shallow as he lifted his head and looked down at her breasts.

They were small but perfectly shaped, the crests a deep, dusty color, and they were puckered, begging for his touch. He lifted the mounds in his hands, feeling their soft weight, stroking and caressing her before delicately circling one nipple with his thumb and forefinger.

When she made a small, needy sound, he bent to the other side, imitating the action with his tongue.

She moved against him, her hands sliding up and down his back, over his shoulders, splaying themselves against his hot skin. Then her fingers moved upward, through his hair, and clasped his head, pulling him closer.

Accepting the invitation, he took her into his mouth,

stroking and sucking while he used his hand on the other breast.

He was so hot he thought he might set the bed on fire. And she seemed equally aroused.

It was impossible not to move his hips against her now. Impossible not to picture himself stripping off her shorts so he could touch her intimately.

His hand cupped her hip, and that was when her fingers grabbed his.

"Max...no," she said, the words high and broken.

He raised his head and looked down at her, trying to make sense of what she'd just said. She wanted him as much as he wanted her. He was sure of that. But she was telling him to stop.

"Why not?" he asked, hearing the thickness of his own voice.

"Because it's wrong. I mean...people aren't supposed to do this."

Certainly not on such short acquaintance, he thought. He knew that he'd let his own needs push him toward something dangerous. He still didn't know if he could trust this woman, yet he was getting ready to make love with her. And that could be a bad mistake. He was already too emotionally involved. Lord, he'd even wondered what he'd do if her needs conflicted with his job.

"You're right," he growled, rolling onto his back and grabbing up a wad of bedding as he struggled to get his body under control.

After half a minute, he heaved himself off the bunk and started down the hall. Then he remembered the gun he left on the floor. Nice work, Dakota!

As much as he hated returning to her room, he couldn't leave the weapon there. Reluctantly he stalked back to her cabin, ignoring her wide-eyed stare as he snatched up the Glock and departed again, thinking that he'd never acted with less professionalism in his damn life.

He was sure he couldn't sleep now. He was too hot, too needy and too confounded by his own behavior. He'd never gotten involved with a woman this quickly. Not even Stephanie. Relationships had never been easy for him. Maybe that was why he'd liked the spy business. You had an excuse for not getting close. But Stephanie had been in the same profession. Their common experiences helped forge a bond between them.

Was that happening with Annie? He recognized a fellow misfit spook and was reaching out to her.

Somehow, after that, he did sleep, and he awoke again with a start. Again he heard Annie's voice. This time she was outside. And this time she wasn't alone. She was speaking to a man who sounded all too familiar.

Bert Trainer.

Every muscle in Max's body tensed. He'd wondered if she was playing some kind of game with Trainer. Now it looked as if she'd sneaked out to meet the sheriff.

To make a report? Was that what this was all about? While he'd been trying to get her to accept his help, she'd been figuring out the best way to tell her friends what she'd learned about Max Dakota, the prize fool in the big boat.

He cursed under his breath. At the same time he racked his brain, trying to think if he'd let slip any information the bad guys in town could use.

Chapter Seven

Max pulled on a pair of shorts and shrugged into one of his aloha shirts, resisting the urge to bring the Glock along. That would be a dangerous move.

As he hurried barefoot up the companionway, he buttoned the shirt.

Through the windows of the lounge, in the glow from one of the overhead dock lights, he spotted two pairs of legs. The sheriff was wearing his usual dark pants and trooper boots. Annie's legs were bare. But he could see she had finally put on the sandals he'd given her. They were at least two sizes too large for her feet, and he couldn't stop himself from making a mental note to get her some that fit better. Damn. Why was he worrying about her shoes? Especially if he was going to be kicking her butt off the boat. That is, if he didn't end up in a jail cell—or in the swamp.

Then the sheriff's words filtered through to him.

"Tell me again how you happened to be sneaking around the dock at three in the morning," Trainer was saying.

"I'm not sneaking around. I...I'm a guest of Max Dakota, and I came out here to get some fresh air."

"Uh-huh," Trainer said, as if he didn't believe a

word. As if he had never met her before and was doing his damnedest to find out who she was. "You plannin' to go down to Nicki's Paradise and get some more fresh air?" the lawman asked.

"What is…what's that supposed to mean?" Annie parried, obviously trying to keep up with the conversation.

"You tell me, missy."

Max waited to hear what she said, remembering that he'd mentioned the nightclub to her.

She didn't say anything.

"Cat got your tongue, missy?" Trainer asked.

She still said nothing, and Max wondered if she understood the question, given her previous reactions to American idioms.

"I think you and me are going to take a trip to the station house where we can have a nice, cozy chat. What you can do to help yourself here, missy, is you can tell me what your boyfriend is up to."

Max waited tensely for what she might say. Then he saw Annie shift her weight from one foot to the other and felt his own muscles turn to hard knots. He had come to know Annie's body language all too well, and that little movement told him a lot. She wasn't planning on going down to any station house. She was going to try the same thing on the sheriff that she'd tried on him. Attack and escape. But it seemed she didn't know that Trainer was likely to shoot her in the back when she turned to make her getaway.

Unless the sheriff wanted information from her. It didn't sound as if she was in on the Hermosa Harbor drug deal, but he couldn't be sure. She could have been working with Trainer and decided she wanted out. When they'd concluded she was defecting, they'd tried to get rid of her. Now they were offering to let her go if she ratted on Max Dakota.

Only, she didn't have enough information to do much damage in that department. Or did she? He'd thought she was asleep while he'd been at the computer. But she could have been prowling the boat, looking for stuff she could use against him. Was there anything she could have found that would link him to Light Street? Or to Jamie Jacobson?

Damn. He knew he should have been more careful about letting his emotions overcome his good sense. He knew he'd been operating in that mode for a while now, but the difference this time was that he'd let himself get wound up with Annie.

As those thoughts whirled in his head, he hurried up the companionway and onto the deck, then slowed his pace as he came in sight of the two people on the dock.

"Honey, there you are," he said in the easy drawl he'd been using since he'd arrived in Hermosa Harbor. "I woke up and you weren't in bed. And when you weren't up in the lounge getting a glass of hot milk, I wondered where you'd gone."

Annie goggled at him. When she didn't answer, he turned to Trainer. "Is there some problem, Sheriff?"

Obviously both surprised and annoyed, the lawman swung around to give Max a considering look. "This lady claims to be a friend of yours. Is that accurate?"

"A very good friend," Max said, keeping his voice calm and his stride easy as he moved across the deck. No use letting the opposition know that his dry mouth was making it difficult to speak.

He waited while a little swell made the boat sway, then climbed over the side and onto the dock. He noted Annie's wide eyes and rigid stance as he sauntered over to her. When he slung his arm around her shoulder, he could feel the tautness in her body. As much to calm himself as to calm her, he stroked his hand up and down her arm, over the goose bumps that dotted her skin. Not from cold, he assumed, because the Florida night was balmy.

He made a tsking noise, as though speaking to a naughty child. "Honey, you should let me know when you're planning to disappear on me in the middle of the night. I was worried. And it looks like Sheriff Trainer was worried, too."

She gave a tight nod. Trainer flicked an assessing glance from Annie to him and back again. He knew the sheriff caught the way she swallowed nervously.

"She wouldn't tell me her name," the lawman said.

"Well, Bert Trainer, meet Annie…Oakland," he said, pausing just a beat when it occurred to him that Annie Oakley was going to sound like a joke.

"I'd like to see some identification," Trainer said.

Panic bloomed on her face, so Max answered for her. "Unfortunately, her purse went over the side when the boat gave a lurch. She lost her driver's license and all her credit cards."

Trainer folded his arms across his chest and shot her a doubtful look. "Is that so?"

"Yes," she agreed quickly.

"Kind of inconvenient."

"You've got that right!" Max answered. "We'll have to send for duplicates."

"From where?"

"Well, she lives in Maryland. Outside Baltimore."

"Address?"

Max cursed silently, wishing he hadn't started manufacturing details. With an inward shrug, he gave his own address in Ellicott City.

Trainer wrote it down.

"You'd best not do any driving until you get a duplicate license."

"Yes. Thank you for the advice," Annie said, moving closer to Max.

"How exactly did you get here?" Trainer asked.

This time Max was the one who drew a blank. As he scrambled for an answer, Annie spoke up briskly.

"Max picked me up in Twin Rivers," she answered, naming a town just to the north of them up the Florida coast. Good going, he thought.

Before Trainer could ask another question, Annie cleared her throat. "I probably should go back to bed," she said.

"Good idea," Max agreed, stroking her arm again before giving Trainer a direct look. "Thanks for taking such good care of my lady."

"Don't mention it," the sheriff answered, a definite edge in his voice. With his arm around Annie, Max felt a small shiver go through her.

"Let's go get comfortable, sweetie pie," he said, hoping he wasn't overdoing the endearments. Really, he was angry enough to strangle her, but it could be a fatal mistake to let Trainer know that.

Feeling the lawman's eyes boring into his back, he escorted Annie onto the deck, then waited with her while Trainer's footsteps receded slowly down the dock in the direction of the parking lot.

Without looking back, Max tightened his hold on Annie's arm and led her back into the lounge.

Not until he'd closed the door behind them did he

turn to her with his eyes flashing. "What the hell were you doing out there?" he asked, keeping his voice low.

She raised her chin. "I had to leave."

"And just where did you think you were going?"

"I…" She stopped, shrugged.

"If I hadn't come out there, your buddy Trainer would have hustled you off in his patrol car. And I'm not so sure you would have ended up at the station house."

"He's not my buddy," she said.

"Are you sure of that? He seemed pretty interested in you. He seemed as if he might know you."

"Where did you get that impression?"

"From your conversation," he pressed, even though he didn't know exactly how to interpret the conversation.

"No."

"Then what?" he shouted, angry with himself for losing his cool.

Her face crumpled, and he felt a stab of guilt. She'd just had a very nasty, very close call. Struggling to speak slowly and distinctly, he said, "How do you know you're not best pals, since you claim you can't remember anything?"

"We have covered that ground before, I think," she said defiantly. "When are you going to believe me?"

"When you start coming clean with me."

"Coming clean?"

"Telling the truth!"

"I am."

"Really? If you don't remember anything, where did you get the name of Twin Rivers?"

"I looked on a map and saw it."

"Yeah, right."

"I have excellent map-reading skills."

He dragged in a breath and let it out in a rush. "Okay, let's play it your way. You don't know Hermosa Harbor. You don't know what you're doing here. But you think you're just going to leave the boat—and go do what?"

She shrugged again.

"Well, maybe you'll be thinking more clearly in the morning." He regarded her for several moments, wondering what the hell he was going to do. One thing for sure, he couldn't trust her to stay put.

"If I were smart, I'd just let you go. Then you'd be someone else's problem. But I have the feeling that you wouldn't get very far. So we're going to try a quick fix. In the morning we'll regroup."

He was speaking as much for his own benefit as hers while he led her belowdecks once more.

The fight seemed to have gone out of her. She didn't protest as he marched her down the hall to his room, where he turned his back on her so she couldn't see what he was taking out of a drawer. Then he escorted her to the cabin where she'd been sleeping earlier. Or maybe she never had been sleeping. Maybe she'd just been lying in there waiting for him to drift off so she could make her escape.

"Lie down," he said, gesturing toward the bunk.

She did so, staring up at him with an unreadable expression.

In one smooth motion, he slipped a handcuff onto her right wrist. Its mate went around the metal chain that held up the bunk.

She gasped, pulling at her hand, then letting it fall back to her side. "No!"

"Sorry. But I need to get some sleep, and it's obvious

that I can't trust you to stay put. And I need to know what you were planning to take with you when you decided to bail out.''

As he spoke, he moved his hands expertly over her body. Into her pocket he found one of the steak knives from the galley.

Liberating it, he tossed it onto the desk.

She looked up at him with large, wounded eyes as he kept searching, and he saw that she was the one who felt betrayed. That gave him a twinge, but he stayed on task. In the other pocket, he felt the slippery surface of a plastic bag.

She hadn't grabbed for the knife, but she grabbed for the little package. The cuffs stopped her, and she was forced to crouch in an awkward position before easing back onto the bed.

''What's this? Your drug stash?'' he asked, stepping out of her reach, disappointment making his tone harsh. ''What are you on, honey? Uppers? Downers? Is that what's causing your mood swings? Or maybe you've fried your brains and now you're trying to figure out how to get your head out of your ass?''

''No!''

He held up the bag, trying to see the contents. As far as he could tell, there was a piece of paper inside. Which was how LSD was packaged. Drops of the stuff dripped onto absorbent paper. ''What is it? Acid?''

''Give that back to me,'' she said, unable to hide the note of panic in her voice.

''Not a chance.''

Moving to the desk, he turned on the light and held up the bag. She'd sealed it with tape. He opened it carefully, keeping one eye on her, watching the desperate set of her features as he pried off the tape, extracted the paper and unfolded it.

Tension radiated from her like a stove burner on high as he stared down at the sheet. There were no telltale dots. Instead, in the middle of the paper someone had drawn a symbol he didn't recognize. A circle with an X through it.

"What the hell is this supposed to mean?" he asked.

She didn't answer, but she kept her gaze pinned to him.

He ran a hand through his hair. "Something from a biker gang? A symbol for your distributor so he'll know you? A message to your mom?" He laughed as he delivered the last line.

Apparently she didn't think it was funny. "No," she clipped out.

"Then what is it?" he shouted, somehow keeping himself from crossing the room, taking her by the shoulders and shaking her.

Again she pressed her lips together. Apparently she didn't know how close he was to physical violence.

"Why is it so important?" he pressed.

She only shrugged.

"You say you can't remember anything, but this thing is apparently important to you!"

As he struggled to hold himself together, he silently admitted that he didn't know why he was so angry, except that he felt he'd been conned. And he shouldn't—because he hadn't known this woman long enough to form an emotional attachment. That was what he told himself, but deep down he understood that he didn't believe it.

"Get some sleep," he advised. "I'm ready to strangle you now, but maybe I'll be more rational in the morning."

THE LATE-NIGHT ENCOUNTER on the dock had shaken Bert Trainer. There was something about the woman who called herself Annie Oakland that set his teeth on edge.

She'd been tough. But she'd been afraid of him, and he would have gotten some information out of her if Max Dakota hadn't picked the wrong time to show up.

They were up to something—and he was going to find out what. He didn't like the way she'd suddenly appeared in town. He wanted to know why.

He pulled his cruiser into the drive-in lane at an all-night burger joint and ordered a greasy, double bacon cheeseburger. And a chocolate milk shake. Junk food. Rich and satisfying.

Then he drove home to the house he'd bought with his ill-gotten gains. He had a nice little racket going with Nicki Armstrong. She scratched his back, and he watched out for her. A very comfortable arrangement.

When he'd first gotten to south Florida, he'd been a fish out of water. It had taken some time for him to settle into a reasonable lifestyle. But he'd always been tough as alligator hide. And a quick study. He loved it here now with a passion that bordered on obsession.

But he was always waiting—waiting for something or someone to come along and screw it all up.

He carried his food out to the deck that overlooked the swamp. Nature in the raw. He could never get enough of the earthy smells wafting toward him in the breeze.

Settling into a comfortable rocking chair, he set his meal on the side table, then opened the bag and began to eat. Not too fast—he wanted to savor the taste of the greasy food and the shake. The folks here didn't know how good they had it. But he did, and he was hoping his luck was going to hold.

BACK IN HIS ROOM, Max was careful not to slam the door. After closing it carefully, he sat down at the desk and booted up his computer.

First he did a web search for the symbol on the piece of paper. He'd been correct. It was the insignia from a biker gang—the Hell Raisers—centered in upper New York State. So why would they send someone down to Hermosa Harbor?

He didn't know the answer. He also didn't know why Annie wrapped the damn symbol in a plastic bag and sealed it up. Was she planning to get on another boat with it and wanted to make sure it didn't get wet? Was she planning to leave it for someone? Maybe it didn't have anything to do with the biker gang. Maybe it was some kind of code she was using to tell her friends she'd made contact with Max Dakota.

But for what reason? Were they planning to hijack *The Wrong Stuff*? Kidnap him?

He bit back a curse. There was no way of figuring it out. Not without applying some pressure on her.

Maybe he'd better do what he'd suggested to her— get some sleep. He wasn't exactly thinking straight right now, and he had the feeling he was going to need his wits about him when he saw her in the morning.

He thought about getting undressed again. Instead, he decided to keep his clothing on, just in case.

Next he picked up the piece of paper and slipped it back into the plastic bag. He was about to put it into his desk drawer when he changed his mind. It could be important, and in that case he'd better put it somewhere secure.

He slid aside the picture on the bulkhead behind his bunk and unlocked the small safe hidden behind it. After slipping the paper inside, he lay down. But he couldn't stop thinking about the woman. He'd been so focused on the incident with Trainer and the symbol on the piece of paper that he'd forgotten about what had happened earlier. She'd been dreaming, talking in her sleep. And then afterward, when her guard was down, she'd told him some interesting stuff.

She'd spoken of a sister, Suli, which was an odd name. She'd spoken of a brute named Angelo. It sounded as if he'd physically abused her.

He had no way of knowing if that was true. Either she'd been revealing facts from her life, or she was living in some sort of fantasy world.

He closed his eyes, willing his mind to sleep.

He woke up when it was still dark. In the light from the companionway, he saw that Annie was leaning over his desk, rifling through one of the drawers.

But he'd left her handcuffed to her bunk. He blinked. Was he dreaming?

"What the hell?" he said.

At the sound of his voice, she whirled, and he saw that she was holding the Glock—leveled at his chest.

Chapter Eight

This was no dream. Max was wide awake and staring down the barrel of his own gun.

Trying to ignore the inconvenient fact that the woman across the room could blow him away with a twitch of her trigger finger, he said, "I thought I cuffed you to the bunk. How did you get loose?"

"I opened the lock."

"How?"

She shrugged. "I just did it."

"Okay." He wet his dry lips, then asked the sixty-four-thousand-dollar question. "And now are you planning to kill me?"

At least the question seemed to cause her some mental anguish, judging from the expression that flickered over her face. "I don't want to. You...saved my life."

"Yeah. A point in my favor," he said, keeping his voice even. He'd always thought of himself as a good poker player. Now he was playing the game of his life.

He sat up in bed and put his feet on the floor. He and Annie stared at each other across several yards of charged space. Too bad she held the boss hand.

"I'd suggest you put down the gun before we have an accident here."

"I'm familiar with the operation of this weapon," she said, sounding as if she was repeating a lesson she'd recently learned. But then, a lot of what she said sounded that way.

Somehow he wasn't reassured.

"I can't put down the gun," she added. "I can't trust you. Not after you chained me to the bed like…like a dime girl."

"A what?"

She blinked as though she'd just realized what she'd said. "A dime girl. You don't know what that is?"

"Enlighten me."

"Dime girls don't have anywhere else to go, so they, you know, service men. But sometimes they want to leave, so…" She shrugged.

Max knew a lot of slang expressions, but he'd never heard of a dime girl. He'd have to ask her about it, when he wasn't in danger of having her drill a hole in his chest.

"Put the gun down," he said again.

She shook her head. "I have to get out of here."

"And do what?"

"I looked through the desk. The piece of paper you took from me is not there."

"Too obvious," he agreed, glad he'd taken the precaution of using the safe. Maybe the paper could be a bargaining chip for his life.

"Where is it?"

He shrugged. "What if I flushed it down the toilet?"

"I can make another one."

"Then why are you looking through my desk?"

"There may be other things here."

"Like what?"

"That is none of your business."

"Sure. You're none of my business." Despite the gun, he glared at her. "Get off the boat. I'll even give you some money if you haven't already stolen some from me. Go on. Be my guest. Give it your best shot. You said you had something important to do, but I wouldn't lay odds that you'll be able to do it."

As he spoke, he watched her face, seeing the uncertainty, knowing that on some level he was getting through to her, so he kept pushing—hard. "Somebody trained you for a secret mission. But you can't remember what it is. What do you think you're going to do—wander around town until something looks familiar?"

She had broken down before, after the nightmare. Now he knew she was holding herself together with spit and baling wire.

"I know you're trying to act tough," he continued. "Hell, you *are* tough. You've handled yourself well in situations that would reduce most women—and most men—to a quivering mass of jelly. But you've handled it."

"No," she said, her voice hardly a whisper. "I'm making a total mess of everything. Last night…last night I knew that man, Sheriff Trainer, wanted to hurt me. You stopped him."

She looked so utterly lost, so utterly bewildered. Like a small child who'd found out her parents had been killed in a car accident.

He fought to shake that image out of his head as he came off the bed. "Put down the gun."

She set it carefully on the desk.

He wasn't sure what he had meant to do, but he found himself gathering her to him, wanting to give her comfort, even after she'd given him a good scare. He felt the desperation in her as he combed his fingers through her hair, stroked her shoulder.

"It will be all right," he soothed, marveling at his own unstable emotions. She might have been holding a gun on him less than a minute ago, but now he was thinking about tipping her face up to his and kissing her. Yet he didn't. Some part of him knew that it was important to demonstrate that he could hold her and not have it turn sexual. He understood that was vital now, even if he wasn't absolutely sure why.

"I'm supposed to be competent," she whispered. "I'm supposed to be able to handle myself."

He made a strangled sound, because he'd once encountered another woman who'd said the same thing. "That attitude is what got my wife killed."

"Oh. I'm sorry. Your parents. Then your wife, too. What happened?"

He sighed. "About all I can tell you is that we were on a covert operation. Stephanie made a grandstand play, and it came out badly."

She gave a tight nod.

"I was with the government. And I can't talk about my past because of the nature of the work." He paused, knowing he'd come to a decision. In an even voice, he went on, "I shouldn't talk about what I'm doing now. But I will, because maybe it will help you understand where I'm coming from. I'm not just down here in Hermosa Harbor relaxing in the sun like the locals are supposed to think. I work for a private investigative agency now. I was sent down here to look into the death of a young man. Apparently he was mixed up in a drug-smuggling operation. When he got out of line or asked too many questions, they left him facedown in the swamp."

He watched her take it in. "So you can see why I have to be cautious. I'm betting Sheriff Trainer is in on it. Also that woman who called me on the phone—Nicki Armstrong. And Hap Henderson is part of it, too. They tend to eliminate people who get in their way."

"Why are you telling me all this?"

"I'm hoping that if I'm absolutely straight with you, you'll be straight with me."

He didn't push for an instant answer, but he was praying they had turned some kind of corner. "Let's go to the galley. You can think about it over some vanilla ice cream with butterscotch syrup."

"Over what?"

"You've never heard of butterscotch syrup over vanilla ice cream?"

"I have heard of ice cream."

"Yeah, well, it's right up there with the American flag and motherhood."

The joking comment only made her look grave. "The American flag has a field of blue with stars in the upper left-hand corner. The rest is red and white stripes."

"You sound like you memorized that in a classroom."

"Maybe I did," she said in a small voice.

"Well, let's take vanilla ice cream and butterscotch into the realm of real experience."

THE CLUB WAS CLOSED for the night when Nicki Armstrong's phone rang.

She'd already gotten a report from Trainer. Was it him again? She snatched up the receiver. "Hello?"

"Are you waiting for a crate of Vidalia onions?" a voice asked.

It wasn't Trainer on the other end of the line. It was

someone she didn't know. But she recognized the onion reference. It was a code she'd been told to expect.

"We have onion soup on the menu next week," she said.

"Then you'll want to take delivery tomorrow night."

"Wait—"

Before she could finish her sentence, the man on the other end of the line cut the connection.

She waited for her heart to stop pounding. Until a few weeks ago, she'd had a nice little operation going in Hermosa Harbor. Until Max Dakota had started poking around. He'd tried to make it look as if he was simply having a good time down here. But she'd bet it was just a cover. She might not have any proof yet, but she felt it in her gut. And now she would have liked to postpone the latest drug delivery. Unfortunately, the timetable wasn't hers.

Picking up the phone again, she dialed Hap.

"Anything new?" she asked.

"They're still holed up in the boat. I can see them in the galley. I think they're making ice-cream sundaes."

She snorted. "How quaint. Let me know if they go out again."

"You know I will."

She kept the phone in her hand, thinking that Max Dakota was a loose cannon she couldn't afford. She needed to know whose side he was on. To that end, she called one of the men in town who helped her out on occasion and gave him explicit instructions.

ANNIE WATCHED Max scoop two mounds of white stuff into bowls. The ice cream. She had heard of it but never tasted any. After spooning sticky golden goo on top, he carried the bowls to the table, putting one in front of his place and one in front of hers. He stuck his spoon in the messy-looking stuff and carried it to his mouth.

She imitated what he'd done, knowing he was watching her.

The first sensation she had was cold, like the iced tea but colder. Then what took her by storm was the burst of flavor in her mouth.

"Oh!"

She stared down at the bowl in wonder. He had taken blobs of cold white stuff and poured on something that looked like grease and produced a combination that filled her mouth with pleasure.

She spooned up another bite of the magic food he had called a butterscotch sundae, sure that she had never tasted anything like it in her life.

"This is—" she stopped, fumbled for the right word "—bully."

"Bully?"

"Good. Very good."

She saw him lean back in his chair, his expression thoughtful. "Bully," he said slowly. "I read a biography of Theodore Roosevelt once. That was a word he used."

"I don't know why I used that adjective. It just popped into my head."

"Yeah. Well, it hasn't been in style for the past eighty years or so."

They were both silent for several moments. She lifted the spoon again and savored the sweet, smooth taste. She couldn't stop herself from running her tongue over her lips to catch every delicious bit.

Looking up, she found Max watching her and she flushed. "I guess I'm being impolite."

"Well, it wouldn't do if you were having tea with the queen of England. But it's okay on *The Wrong Stuff*."

The queen of England. Was she likely to meet that lady in a small town in Florida? The question made her brain feel muzzy, the way it often had since Max had pulled her out of the water. She would try to figure something out, and she'd feel as if fog was choking off her thought processes.

Max was speaking again, and she struggled to focus on his words. "So now that I've impressed you in the food department again, maybe you'll tell me what you drew on that piece of paper. Maybe you'll even let me help you."

She had been bitterly afraid to trust this man. But something had changed after she'd held the gun on him.

When she had put down the weapon, he might have killed her, or at the very least punished her. Instead, incredibly, he had hugged her, then brought her up to the galley for the most amazing thing she had ever tasted. And in those simple acts of kindness, he had shattered her defenses. She wanted to answer him honestly now.

"I don't know what I drew."

"Then how did you draw it?" he asked immediately.

"I just...picked up a pencil and drew."

"Oh, yeah?" He sounded frustrated.

"I'm not lying to you," she said. Well, not exactly. The mark was branded into her brain and tattooed on her body.

Her words came faster as she continued, "I know it's important. I know I'm supposed to leave it at a building downtown. I can picture the spot. But I don't know why I'm supposed to do it."

"Okay."

"You still think I'm...not coming clean," she said, trying to fight the defeated feeling that threatened to swamp her.

"You have to admit that explanation is a little harder to swallow than ice cream with butterscotch sauce. What building?"

So much in her mind was misty. But the building and the mark were very clear. "It's big and white. A very solid structure. Massive. But it's not tall." She paused for a moment, then added, "And you cross a big plaza to get to the front entrance. There's a gate. And flags out front."

He thought for a minute, apparently taking an inventory of the large structures in town. "Fort De Leon? The old Spanish fort downtown?"

"Maybe."

"Why there?"

"Because it has been standing a long time. Because it won't get wiped out in the flood," she told him, wondering how she knew that part.

"Yeah, it was built on high ground—or high by Florida standards. And it's got walls three feet thick. I guess it would withstand high water, if this place were going to flood. What else do you know about that?"

She blinked. "I don't know specifically. But anyone who has studied the weather changes over the past few years knows that a lot of coastal communities are going to be underwater. Especially on a peninsula that sticks out into the ocean and the Gulf of Mexico."

"Have you studied weather changes?"

She shrugged, then took another swallow of the sundae, more like a gulp.

"I can see this discussion is making you uncomfortable." Max's tone was sympathetic.

She nodded. "I want to answer your questions, but I can't. I feel like my chest is so tight that I can hardly breathe. I have to take that paper down there and leave it in a specific spot. After I do that, I think I'll feel better."

"You're making it sound as if you've been given a posthypnotic suggestion."

"What does that mean?" she asked carefully, afraid she might already know the answer.

"It's possible to put a person in a hypnotic trance and make suggestions about what she's supposed to do. Then she does it."

"Like what?"

He shrugged. "They use it in nightclub acts sometimes. You get a person up on the stage, hypnotize him, then tell him that when the band starts playing a certain song, he'll get up and start prancing like a chicken or something just as weird. Everybody in the room is waiting for it to happen, so they laugh when he does it just as he was told."

She sat there, clutching the cold bowl, trying to picture the scene he was describing. He'd said too many things that didn't quite make sense to her. But if she started asking for clarification, they would be sitting at the table for hours.

"Would you take me to the Fort De Leon?" she asked.

"Yes."

"Thank you!"

"But maybe we could try something else first."

"What?"

"I have some specialized training. Would you let me

hypnotize you and see if we can get your memory back?''

She raised her eyes to his face, studying his features. Allowing him do that would be taking a terrible risk. She would be opening herself up to letting him control her. At least that was what it sounded like from what he'd said about the nightclub act.

But she was almost desperate enough to take the leap off the cliff. Almost.

She licked her suddenly dry lips. ''What guarantee do I have that you won't try to...hurt me...control me?''

''No guarantee. You have to trust me. But that's been the issue all along, hasn't it?''

Chapter Nine

Could she trust him? Until this morning she had fought him every step of the way because some deeply buried commandment that had decreed she trust no one. Now tight fear clogged her throat, making it almost impossible to breathe.

Max's actions had spoken eloquently in his favor. True, he had cuffed her to her bunk, but he had not hit her. He had never hurt her—even when she'd tried to kill him.

But then there was her basic problem. Since she'd arrived in Hermosa Harbor, she had been operating on pure nerves, trying to accomplish some mission that she couldn't even remember. Which meant that putting herself in this man's power was a foolish step to take. She should refuse.

Long seconds passed as her mind scrambled in circles, trying to decide. Finally, she drew in a shuddering breath, then raised her chin. "All right. Do what you have to."

She'd thought he would look triumphant, or relieved. Instead, he pressed her with another question. "You're sure?"

Her own anxiety leaped up. "No! I'm not sure of

anything. You had better do it before I change my mind.''

''Okay,'' he answered, but he didn't sound entirely convinced.

''You suggested it. Are you backing out?''

''No. I'm considering whether this is the best thing for you.''

''A minute ago, you said it was.''

''That's when I was trying to get you to say yes. Now I'm thinking it through.''

''Carp!''

He laughed. ''Well, if you put it that way, let's roll.''

''What are we going to roll?''

He gave her a strange look. ''You don't know that famous phrase? From 9-11.''

''I know 9-11.'' She felt chilled to the bone.

In her mind, she pictured two impossibly tall buildings. Two airplanes. Blinking, she focused on Max again. He was standing up, looking around the room, then out the window.

''There's really no good place to do this. There's no privacy in this damn marina. Let me give you a choice. We can drive out to the highway and rent a motel room.''

''A bedroom?''

''Yes. Or we can go below.''

''If we go below, where will we do it?''

''My cabin.''

She thought about that. Either way, she was going to be alone in a bedroom with him. Putting herself in his power. If she was going to do that, it better be quickly, before she lost her nerve.

''Your cabin,'' she said, letting him lead the way.

He stopped in the doorway of his room. ''You should

really be sitting in a comfortable chair. So should I, but I guess we can use the bed.''

He started straightening the covers, and she moved to the other side of the mattress, helping him, trying to hide the shaking of her hands. He piled pillows against the headboard, then came around the bed and reached for her, folding her against him, stroking his hands up and down her arms.

''We don't have to do this.''

''Stop giving me the chance to back out. You've offered to help me find out who I am and why I'm here. I have to take the chance. Then maybe I'll have to leap off the bed and assault you.''

''Did you just make a joke?''

''I hope so,'' she answered.

''Okay.'' He took a step back, turning her loose, and she immediately missed the warmth of his body. ''Sit on the bed. Make yourself comfortable.''

She did as he asked, feeling the stiffness of her muscles as she worked her back against the pillows.

He moved around the room, closing the gaps in the curtains, then turning on the lamp in the corner. When he leaned his hips against the ledge of the built-in dressers across from the bed, she could see he was also tense.

To break the silence she asked, ''What should I do? Close my eyes?''

''No. Look up to the line where the ceiling meets the bulkhead.''

She raised her eyes, focusing on that spot.

''Are you comfortable?''

''Yes,'' she answered, because she was trying to make herself so.

''Relax,'' he said. ''Everything is all right. You're going to let yourself relax. You're going to feel very good. Just listen to the sound of my voice and let your mind drift.''

His voice was low and soothing; it was easy to listen to. "You're feeling sleepy. You're feeling very good. I want you to relax now. Relax now.''

She settled farther into the pillows.

"Are you relaxed?''

"Yes," she whispered because magically she was feeling much calmer than she had a few minutes earlier. She didn't know why his voice and the setting were having that effect, but whatever he was doing was working.

"Close your eyes if you want to.''

She did.

"You're going to a safe place. A place you'd like to be. Where is that?''

"The caves," she answered, feeling a wave of longing sweep over her. She wanted to be back there. Safe and sound.

"Yes. Good. What are the caves?''

She tried to tell him. "They're warm and secure. You can sleep there. The danger is outside.''

"Good. You're warm and safe in the caves. Are you feeling good?''

"Yes.''

"Enjoy the caves.''

She smiled and nodded.

"Can you tell me more about the caves?''

"No!'' The tension was back in her body.

"Okay. It's all right. You don't have to tell me about it. You're warm and safe there.''

"Yes," she agreed. But it was not quite the same now.

"Can you tell me your name?'' he asked suddenly.

She started to answer, then knew she was not supposed to say. "No."

"Why not?"

"I'm not allowed to." The feeling of danger increased, and she wanted to be back where she was warm and safe.

Maybe her expression had given her away, because he said, "You don't have to tell me anything."

"Yes," she answered, but she sensed danger coming closer. A pain had started in her head. It grew quickly, overwhelming her, making it difficult to think.

The walls of the cave seemed to close in around her, choking off her breath. She heard a groaning sound and knew that it had come from her own lips.

"What is it?" Max asked anxiously.

"It hurts."

"What?"

"My head. It feels like it is going to explode." It was true. The pressure inside her skull was more than she could bear.

"Annie."

"I'm not Annie!" she cried. Another name floated just out of her reach, and she tried to grab it and pull it closer. But then it was washed away in a wave of agony.

"Who are you?" he asked, his voice urgent.

She knew the answer to the question. Again she tried to speak, but the pain overwhelmed her, blotting out everything else, so that the memory slid away.

"Annie, wake up. Wake up now."

"I…" Her body jerked, and she cried out.

When she opened her eyes, Max was beside her on the bed. He'd pulled her into his arms and was holding her tightly.

"My head hurts so much," she whispered.

"Annie, I'm so sorry," he murmured, his lips close to her ear.

She clung to him, fighting the pain, thinking she was going to throw up all that nice ice cream and make a mess of herself and the bed and him. But she fought to keep the food down and gradually the sick feeling and the pain in her head receded to a level where she could function. Opening her eyes, she looked around at her surroundings. She was with Max. On his boat. "I was somewhere else."

"Where?"

"The caves."

"Can you tell me about it?"

"I…" She tried to describe the place better, but the pain came zinging back to her, cutting off her breath.

"What? What's wrong?" he asked urgently.

"Too much pain," she gasped.

He lay her down on the bed, then started to ease away. "Let me get you something."

She clutched at him. "Don't go."

"I'll be right back."

She forced herself to loosen her grip, to lie quietly as he left the room. He returned in a few moments with a glass of water. In his other hand, he held two white tablets.

"This should help," he said.

She could have asked what he was giving her, instead, she took the pills and swallowed them with the water, because now he was the only solid, steady element in a wildly tipping universe. When he sat down on the bed again, she reached for him. After a moment's hesitation, he lay down beside her, gathering her in his arms.

"Max," she said in a broken voice, "what happened to me?"

His face turned hard and angry. "Somebody left a posthypnotic suggestion with you, all right," he replied. "If you get the urge to tell anyone about your past, your head starts to hurt so much that you can't say anything."

"Are...are you sure?"

His hands tightened on her shoulders. "No. I'm not sure of a damn thing. But that's the way it looks from here."

"What can I do about it?"

"I don't know. I've got some limited abilities to put a subject under, but I'm no psychologist. I could take you back to Baltimore. There are people there who could help you."

"No. I can't leave." She sat up, almost overcome with urgency. "And you have a job to do down here," she added quickly.

He sighed. "Yeah." He stroked back a damp lock of her hair. "How do you feel?"

She considered her answer. "Better."

"Good."

She knit her fingers with his free hand and held on tightly. They lay on the bed, wordlessly looking at each other, even as their eyes exchanged a wealth of important information.

There was nothing safe in her life. The cave was far away, where she couldn't climb inside. But this man represented another sort of haven. He could make her forget about the terrible dark cloud that hung over her.

Gently he trailed his finger over her brow, her cheek, the edge of her jaw. "I'd like to choke the bastards who did this to you," he whispered.

"Did what?"

"Stranded you here and made sure you couldn't ask anyone for help."

"Did they take away my memory?"

"I don't know. That part doesn't make sense."

The look of frustration on his face and the deep feeling in his voice tore at her. It sounded as if he cared about her, more than anyone else had ever cared.

Without conscious thought, she lifted her hand and pulled his head down to hers. She squeezed her eyes closed, focusing on the wonderful sensations that always came from the pressure of his mouth against hers.

"Annie?"

She opened her lips, changed the angle of her head, did everything she could to increase the pleasure of the contact.

His mouth was soft against hers, yet hard at the same time. She couldn't understand why that was true, but she loved the feeling.

He rolled her onto her back, pressing her against the mattress as he took control of the kiss, his mouth moving expertly over hers.

She felt something powerful gather in him, which might have frightened her. But she ruthlessly cast any doubts aside and let her own needs rise to meet his.

He was good at what he was doing. His hands and mouth on her felt wonderful. Not just physically, but so much more. This thrilling contact with him had the power to wipe everything else from her mind. There was no need to worry about what she remembered or didn't remember and why. She only had to feel what he was doing to her.

They clung together, rocking slightly. The friction of his body against hers set up vibrations that reached every one of her nerve endings, creating wonderful sensations. Unconsciously she adjusted herself against him, so that the hard shaft at the front of his shorts was wedged against the hot, throbbing place at the top of her legs.

"Max," she gasped, unable to say more.

He lifted his head and looked down at her, his gaze warm with emotions that both exhilarated and frightened her.

With his hips still pressed to hers, he shifted his body so that one of his hands could slide under her shirt. Watching her face, he reached to cover her breast, and she whimpered as he stroked the roundness of her. Her nipples had drawn themselves into tight points, and when he found one and circled it with his finger, she dragged in a strangled breath at the bolt of heat that shot downward through her body.

It was as if there was a channel inside her connecting her breast to that needy place between her thighs. He seemed to know it, too, because he caught her around the hips and pressed her more tightly to himself.

"Good, that's so good," she breathed, hearing the desperate quality in her own voice. She wanted more, but she wasn't sure how to tell him what she wanted. Or if she even should.

But she sensed that he would hold her steady in the dark current that had pulled her under.

When he eased away, she tried to pull him back. Then she saw his hands on the front of her shirt, sliding open one button, then another.

She was reaching to help him get rid of the shirt when a little machine on the bedside table made a screeching noise, and she jumped. Knowing she had been caught doing something wrong, she tried to break away from him.

"What is that?" she gasped.

Max made a disgusted sound. "The clock radio. I'd forgotten I set it. Sorry. I'll shut the damn thing off."

His hand was hovering over the device when a man began to speak only inches from her ear. Phrases leaped out at her, and she grabbed Max's hand.

"What's wrong?" he asked.

"Quiet! Let me listen."

Moments ago she had been totally absorbed in what she and Max were doing. Now the mood was shattered. She focused only on the words.

"Preparations are moving ahead for Governor Robert E. Lee Bradley's visit next week to Sea Kingdom. The Kissimmee High School band will play the state song. Then officials from the park will show him around the new dolphin environment. The newly completed exhibit at Sea Kingdom is expected to attract a significant number of tourists to the state and boost the local economy."

The man switched to another topic, and Annie was left lying on the bed with her heart pounding and her breath coming in small pants.

"What happened? What's wrong?" Max asked again.

"The governor…Sea Kingdom," she said in a strangled voice.

"Yeah, apparently he's visiting there next week. I guess it's a big deal."

He pressed a button on the thing he had called a clock radio, and the voice ceased. She brought her gaze to his and saw him looking at her, an assessing expression on his face.

"What's so important about it?" he asked.

She wanted to climb off the bed and give herself some breathing space, but she stayed where she was and kept her gaze steady. "Something is going to happen," she said in a voice that sounded surprisingly sure. "Something bad."

He sat up and ran a hand through his hair as he looked down at her. Earlier, when he'd held her in his arms, his expression had been like a warm caress, now it was sharp and probing.

She sat up, as well. Ducking her head away from him, she hastily refastened her buttons—partly to give herself time to think.

But Max wasn't going to let her duck the subject. "What do you know about it?" he demanded.

She struggled to sort through her jumbled thoughts. "I… Nothing for certain. But I can't turn off the idea that…something…terrible is going to happen…when he visits the park," she said slowly.

"Like what?" Max pressed, as though by asking the same question again, he could get the answer he wanted. Someone else had done that to her. Another man. But she couldn't remember who.

She shrugged helplessly. "I can't remember."

He cursed softly. "I'd like to know what wiped out your memory." He continued to stare at her, then began to speak. "Okay, how about this? Maybe you're part of a radical group that wants to make a point by killing the governor."

"No! That's not right."

"How do you know, if you can't remember?"

"I would never hurt the governor."

"Maybe that symbol you drew on the piece of paper

is a message to the group. And that's why you have to leave it at the fort.''

She thought about the symbol, the same one that was tattooed under her arm. "No!" she said again, because she didn't want it to be true.

"What makes you so sure? You were ready to kill me. Why not an important official?"

She felt her throat clog, then tried to explain what had happened. "With you I—I panicked. I was trying to get away, not kill you. Deliberately coming here to kill the governor doesn't feel right. Maybe it's the other way round. Maybe I was sent to stop something bad from happening to him.''

"How do you propose to do that?"

"Throw myself in front of him and take a bullet meant for him?"

"No!"

"That's as good a guess as any," she almost shouted.

When she stood up, too frustrated to lie still, so did he.

She wanted to go up to the lounge where she'd have more space. Only, now he was blocking her exit from the small room and there was no way to get around him.

Lifting pleading eyes to his, she said, "I'm sorry if this doesn't make sense to you. I wish it made better sense to me. All I know is that when I heard the name of the governor and the name of the park, I felt…a sense of urgency. I don't know how else to put it."

He sighed. "Okay. We'll assume those feelings are coming from your subconscious, and we should pay attention to them."

She felt herself relax fractionally. "Thank you. Are you going to take me to Sea Kingdom?"

"No. I'm going to call the Light Street Detective Agency."

She tried to grapple with the terrible feeling of disappointment that swept over her.

"What can they do?"

"They can alert the governor's staff. Light Street is a credible source of information, so the security will be increased."

"A credible source of information—unlike me," she couldn't help saying.

"They have government connections. You don't. You don't even know who you are. If you try to tell your story, they're going to take you into custody and interrogate you."

Imagining that made her feel light-headed. "If that happens, I'll die," she whispered.

His gaze drilled into her. "Literally?"

She shrugged. "That's what it makes me feel like," she replied in a whisper.

"Then let me call Light Street."

She didn't like involving them, nor letting Max take charge again, but she gave a tight nod. "Okay, call them."

Max pulled his cell phone out of his pocket and punched in a number. She heard him quickly telling whoever answered the phone that he'd gotten reliable information of a possible attempt on Governor Bradley's life during his visit to Sea Kingdom next week.

There was more discussion, during which he glanced at her several times. Unlike Nicki, the person on the other end of the line this time was speaking in a voice too low to be overheard.

Max had believed her enough to take precautions. But

he had not wiped away the terrible feeling of dread hanging over her.

"I want to go there," she said when he disconnected the call.

"I've got them checking out the park—and the political groups down here."

"That's not enough!"

"Well, we still have almost a week. Let them follow it up. And we can be on the scene if it becomes necessary."

"You would take me there?"

"Yes."

"Why?"

"Because I can see how upset you are. There's something significant for you about the governor's visit to the theme park."

"Thank you," she breathed.

He shifted his weight from one foot to the other, then reached out his hand toward her. But before he touched her, he let the arm fall back again.

"What?" she asked.

"A little while ago, when we were on the bed, you were trying to forget about your mission, weren't you?"

His perceptiveness made her look away to hide the mixture of embarrassment and regret on her face. "What do you mean?" she whispered.

"You didn't want to think about why you were here, so you used me to block it out."

She shrugged, then forced herself to meet his eyes. "That may be true. You can think of it as a moment of weakness on my part. But it's not the only thing that was true. Not the only thing I was feeling."

He answered with a tight nod, and she wanted to tell him that the warmth and closeness she'd experienced with him had meant more to her than she could possibly say. She wanted to tell him that he had triggered monumental changes in her thinking, changes she couldn't fully explain to herself. But she held all that inside, because she wasn't sure it would do her any good. Not with this man. He relied on deeds and actions, not words.

He began speaking again. "About the governor and Sea Kingdom. Why don't you try writing down everything you can think of about the park? See how much you come up with."

She had just been thinking that her behavior would count more with this man than anything she could explain. Now his casually spoken words made goose bumps rise along her arms. All at once she felt trapped. She'd wanted to prove something to him. And he was offering her a way to show him whose side she was on. By doing something that made her feel literally sick to her stomach.

Yet she nodded in agreement, because she hardly had a choice. Not just with him. With herself. She had to find out why she was here, and maybe he had given her a way to do it. There was another benefit, as well. She would have to do it alone—and at the moment she needed to get away from Max.

"There's a pen and paper upstairs. Do you want to sit at the galley table or out on the deck in the sun?"

"Inside," she said quickly, because the thought of being in the open air only made her panic level rise.

Max led her through the lounge, took a pad and pen from one of the drawers along the wall and set them on the table. Then he went out on deck. She could see him through the door, staring out over the water.

She wanted to call him back, to tell him this was a

bad idea. Instead, she turned the pen in her hand, looking at it. It felt oddly heavy, more like a weapon than a writing instrument.

"Stop stalling," she told herself.

With a grimace, she touched the pen to the paper. She had no idea where to start, so she wrote the date of the governor's visit.

March 22.

Then, as though her hand had been taken over by another person, she began to write more.

Chapter Ten

Annie's throat was so dry she could barely swallow. Feeling as if fate had finally caught up with her, she let the pen flow across the paper. It moved quickly. She was writing without even thinking about where the words were coming from and what they might mean. At first it was fairly easy to let the pen carry her hand along.

But as the page filled with writing, it became more and more difficult to make herself continue. All at once, she simply felt too tired to go on. It was a strange sensation, as though her muscles were too weak to hold the pen. She was sure she could never have spoken about what she had just written. But Max's idea of writing, instead of talking, had freed her to do what would have been an impossibility.

Setting the pen down on the table, she dragged in a breath and let it out slowly. When she looked up, she saw Max regarding her gravely. She blinked. "How long have you been there?" she asked.

"A while."

"I didn't see you come in."

"I know. You looked as if you were in a trance—if

you'll pardon the expression. Have you ever heard of automatic writing?''

"No. What is it?"

"When someone claims to communicate with the spirit world and they let the spirit take over and write.''

"Have you seen that?"

"No. But I've heard of it.'' He pulled out the chair opposite her and sat down. "How does your head feel?''

She searched for an answer to the question and came up with a descriptive word. "Empty.''

"No headache?''

She focused on how she felt. "No. Thank The Protectors.''

"The Protectors. Who are they?''

She shook her head. "I wish I knew.''

To break the ensuing silence, she said quickly, "I wrote something.''

"What?''

She glanced down at the paper. "It looks like a lot, but I have no idea what it says.''

"Read it to me,'' he said gently. She wanted to cling to that gentleness, but she wasn't sure it would do her any good. She had gotten close to him a while ago. Now it seemed as if he'd taken a mental step back.

She wanted to crumple the paper into a ball and flush it down the toilet before she found out what she had written. Instead, she picked up the sheet and focused on the handwriting. It didn't even look familiar.

"Sea Kingdom…'' she began, feeling the thickness in her throat. After clearing it, she tried again. "Sea Kingdom occupies two hundred well-landscaped acres in south-central Florida. It is a vacation destination for families from all over the United States but chiefly from the Eastern seaboard. It has never achieved quite the importance of Disney World or Sea World. But it is a major secondary entertainment center. The campus consists of large and small exhibits, as well as parklike areas. All are well maintained. In one building, visitors walk through a plastic tunnel while sharks and other sea creatures swim over them. In another large tank, visitors swim with friendly seagoing mammals called dolphins. In a nearby exhibit, they can watch sea lions perform.

"The penguin house is a climate-controlled habitat where unique, flightless birds frolic in ice-cold water and on snowy cliffs. Nearby is a similar enclosure for polar bears. Killer whales and dolphins perform stunts in a huge amphitheater.

"In a large pool, adults and children can ride in a simulated submarine past displays constructed to resemble coral reefs with fish swimming about.

"The governor will be speaking in the indoor auditorium. The usual activity there is the making of a film where volunteers from the audience can participate in the creation of an underwater rescue movie. Then they can buy the results at a high price."

When Max laughed, she looked up inquiringly.

"It's a good piece of merchandising. The tourists get to take home a flick from vacation where they star with some Hollywood names."

"Oh," she answered, not really understanding. Going back to her text, she read, " 'The governor's appearance will draw dignitaries from all over the state, as well as media from around the world. Which is a crucial part of Carp—' "

What she had written stopped abruptly, and she felt a mixture of relief and frustration.

"Carp," she said. "It says that word, carp."

"Yeah. What does it mean?" he shot at her.

She flapped her arm in an angry gesture. "If I knew, I'd tell you."

He gave her a long look. "It seems you know a lot about Sea Kingdom."

"Yes." She clenched and unclenched her hands. "And before you ask, I don't know why."

"But you went to a lot of trouble to memorize those facts."

"What's your point? What do you want me to do? Just tell me!" Fear and frustration made her shout the plea.

Before he could answer, the phone rang, and she breathed out a small sigh—part relief and part disappointment—as his attention shifted away from her.

For several moments Max listened intently to someone on the other end of the line. Then he said, "Thanks for the information."

When he hung up, she tried to read the expression on his face.

"Who was that?" she asked.

He hesitated and she thought he wasn't going to answer.

"An informant I've cultivated in town." Watching her closely, he added, "He told me that a major drug shipment is going to be delivered tonight. I want to be on hand to document what's happening."

"I will go with you."

"This isn't your concern."

"At the beginning, you thought it was!"

"You know damn well I've changed my mind."

She nodded. That was something, anyway. "Well, you helped me. I want to help you. As you said, I'm good in a fight."

"I don't think there's going to be a fight."

"Let me come with you," she tried again, because it was all she could say.

"What about Sea Kingdom?"

She didn't want to think about Sea Kingdom. In fact, she was glad to have another focus for her attention. "As you pointed out, the governor is not coming until March 22. And you have Light Street working on it."

"Yeah," Max agreed.

"If I'm going with you tonight, we should plan the operation."

"In military terms?"

She shrugged. "If you want to put it that way."

"You're the one who said it."

"And what does that prove?" She struggled to keep her voice level.

It was his turn to shrug.

She swallowed, wondering if she was about to take another terrible chance. "Okay. I see you're still not sure if I'm on your side. Maybe it will help if I show you something I discovered the night I came here."

"What?"

Instead of answering directly, she said, "You mentioned that people can see in through these windows. That they might be watching."

He nodded.

"Then we need to go downstairs."

She got up from the table, and marched toward the stairs without looking back to see if he was following. When she heard his shoes on the treads, she let out the breath she'd been holding.

He followed her inside her cabin, and she turned to face him.

His features were drawn as he asked, "What's the

big secret? Something you found on my boat? Are your friends planning to blow it up?''

Her heart pounded in the back of her throat. "No! It's something on me. Under my shirt, unfortunately."

When he raised an eyebrow, she quickly added, "And I'm not talking about my ta-tas. I didn't bring you down here for a stripper show."

"An interesting choice of words."

"Is it?" she asked, sorry that she was wearing nothing under the shirt. She didn't want to take it off, so with fingers that felt wooden, she lifted the fabric just under her arm and turned so that she was exposing the skin there to his view.

He leaned closer, and she saw from his face the moment he zeroed in on the mark.

His curse zinged along her nerve endings.

"How long have you had that thing?" he demanded.

"I wish I knew. I found it that first day—when I took a shower."

"What the hell is it?"

Ignoring his sharp tone, she tried to keep her own voice even. "You know as much as I do. It looks like the same symbol that I drew on that piece of paper. I didn't know what it meant then and I still don't know."

When she heard him curse again, she cringed, but she wasn't going to just stand there letting him act as if she'd done something wrong. "What? Do you think it's from that biker gang? Do you think I...I belong to them? That they sent me down here for some nefarious purpose and hypnotized me so I couldn't tell anyone about it?"

"I don't know what the carp to think!"

He'd used the word that he'd picked up from her.

And despite the tension, she laughed. "That's a good way to put it."

The laughter died, and they stood regarding each other uneasily. Slowly he raised his hand, and she braced for the contact. His fingers gently touched the tattoo, traced its outline. Holding very still, she struggled to keep her breathing steady. His fingers felt warm against her skin, the way they'd felt when he touched her intimately. But now his purpose was hardly intimate.

"I can feel something under the skin."

"Yes," she whispered.

"What is it?"

Her frustration bubbled over again. "I told you, I don't know! Maybe somebody put a poison capsule there. Maybe I'm supposed to break it when I've completed my assignment."

His hand jumped, and he pulled it quickly away. "You don't really think that, do you?"

"Like you, I don't know what to think."

"But you're tough enough to handle it—whatever it is?"

"I have to be, don't I?"

"Being tough isn't all it's cracked up to be."

She wondered if he was thinking about his wife. She couldn't ask. But the emotion in his voice made her feel exposed, so she let her shirt drop back into place.

They stood together in charged silence. She broke it by clearing her throat and asking, "So now that I've showed you the thing I knew I had to hide at all cost, are you going to let me help you out tonight?"

"If that's what you want to do."

"Yes. Thank you."

His voice became businesslike, and she could tell he

was glad to focus on the assignment. "If you're going, I'd better give you some background. We should make some contingency plans. And I should tell you exactly what we're facing here. Then we need to get you something appropriate to wear."

She nodded in agreement, relieved to turn her attention to the evening ahead and away from the mysterious mark on her body. Away from Sea Kingdom. She was convinced now that it was the reason she was in Florida. But she didn't want to think too much about that. Not yet. She had time, she told herself, even when in her gut she knew that was a lie. Time was her enemy.

MAX LOOKED at Annie sitting across the small table from him and smiled.

She smiled back, but he could tell she didn't like the noise level in Nicki's Paradise, or the flashing lights, or the constant movement of the dancers.

If he had to guess, he'd say she'd never been in a dance club before. Or at least she didn't remember the experience.

For the thousandth time, he wondered about her background. If she'd been a moll in a New York biker gang, the nightclub scene would surely seem familiar.

Had she been raised in a convent? On a Pacific island? In a puritanical cult? And where had she gotten her mixture of ethnic looks, her Scandinavian accent and her stilted way of speaking?

She lifted her glass and took a sip of her soft drink. He'd ordered it for her, suspecting she couldn't handle the hard stuff. To keep his own head clear, he was sticking to soda water with lime.

Partly to fill up the hours before they could leave for the club, they'd gone shopping in the afternoon. He'd enjoyed her delight in what most women he knew would have considered a mundane experience, since they were buying her outfits at a low-end department store out on the highway. She didn't seem to have a woman's instinct for what would look good on her, so he'd helped her make selections. Now she was wearing her favorite—a peach-colored T-shirt with green palm trees and a pair of light-blue jeans, both of which looked a lot better on her than the oversize shirts and shorts she'd borrowed from him.

"We could dance," he said, pitching his voice over the noise.

"I don't know how."

"It's not too difficult. You just move your hips and arms around."

"It looks obscene."

He laughed. "Okay. We don't have to do it."

The conversation came to a halt again. Telling himself that he wanted anyone watching to think they were just here to have a good time, he moved his chair closer to hers and slung his arm around her shoulder. She gave him a quick look, then leaned into him, and he closed his eyes, bending to brush his lips against her cheek, enjoying the contact, pretending for a moment that they were alone.

"Nice to see you." The voice came from behind his head. Jerking around, he saw Nicki Armstrong standing beside their table, staring at them with narrowed eyes. The slender, redheaded nightclub owner must have picked the moment carefully. She folded her arms across her chest.

"Nice to see you, too," he managed to say.

"Where are your manners, Max? Introduce me to your friend."

"Annie Oakland, this is Nicki Armstrong," he said. "Nicki, meet Annie."

"So, you're Max's girlfriend," the standing woman said.

"Yes."

"From up north."

"Baltimore," Annie answered.

"Well, any friend of Max's is a friend of mine," she said, her voice making it clear that the statement was patently false. "Enjoy yourselves," she said, moving off to speak to the couple at the next table.

Beside him, Annie let out a breath.

His arm tightened around her. Lowering his mouth to her ear, he said, "You're doing good."

"She doesn't like me."

"She doesn't like me, either."

Annie gave him a small nod, then took a gulp of her drink. "Maybe I'll go to the ladies' room," she said.

"Sure. I'll be right here."

NERVES REALLY WERE affecting her bladder, Annie thought as she made her way through the crowd toward the sign that said phones and rest rooms. Before they had arrived, Max had explained what a nightclub was like. But his description had hardly prepared her for what she would encounter here. The room was dark and crowded and noisy. It was amazing to think that this was what people considered fun. All she got from this place was a headache and claustrophobia.

Most threatening of all was the woman, Nicki Armstrong. She'd said only a few words to them, but hostility had radiated from her like vapor from a toxic-waste dump.

Annie squeezed past a man and woman who were

standing against the paneled wall kissing and pressing their lower bodies together. And they weren't the only ones. All over the nightclub, couples were kissing and touching in ways that made her blush.

In the ladies' room, she opened one of the stalls and used the toilet. She was about to step out when she heard the rest-room door open and a tense voice say, "I'll watch the door. Check the room. I saw that bitch come down this way." It sounded like Nicki.

In the small cubicle, Annie quickly climbed up on the toilet, then angled her body against the metal wall, prepared to defend herself if she had to. A man pushed the door roughly open and glanced in, but he didn't spot Annie crouching behind the barrier. Still, she didn't let the air out of her lungs until he had walked back toward the rest-room door.

"She's not here."

"Get the cargo put away in the usual place."

The cargo? Max had told her that drug shipments were coming into Hermosa Harbor. Apparently into this nightclub.

"Okay," Nicki said. "If Little Orphan Annie isn't here, she's got to be somewhere. She wouldn't leave lover boy in the lurch. So find that bitch."

The door closed again, and Annie leaned against the stall with her heart pounding. She had to get out of the club. Max had told her there was a rear exit, near the office down the hall. Perhaps she should slip out the back, come around the front and catch Max's attention from the other side of the room.

Opening the rest-room door, she peeked out. The hall was empty. Knowing anything she did was risky, she turned toward the near exit. She was almost to the office when the rear door opened and a man stepped in. It was Sheriff Trainer. He was here!

Because his head was turned and he was talking to someone—another man—he didn't spot her. Pulse pounding in her ears, she dashed back to the ladies' room, squeezing through the door just as a short, dark-haired girl was entering.

Giving Annie a considering look, she asked, "What—are you going to wet your pants?"

"Sorry," Annie managed, stepping back.

As the other woman strode into a stall, Annie looked out the door again. Trainer was just disappearing into the office. Taking the opportunity to escape, she pounded back toward the main room.

WITH A SICK FEELING, she saw she was too late. Max was standing beside the table where they'd been sitting, and another man, bald and burly, was standing close to him. From the tension in Max's shoulders, she was pretty sure he was in a situation he didn't like. But he only looked straight ahead as he let the other guy usher him toward the door.

She strained her eyes in the dim light and saw that the bald man had his hand in the pocket of a light jacket. Did he have a gun in that hand?

As he left the club, he nodded to Nicki, who stood near the door. Her body feigned nonchalance, but her eyes never left the action.

Sure she was trapped, Annie stood indecisively with her heart pounding. But she really had only one option. She dashed back down the hall, expecting at any moment to feel a hand on her shoulder or hear the sheriff ordering her to stop. But she reached the door and breathed out a sigh as she stepped into the humid night air.

Staying close to the side of the building, she moved toward the front of the nightclub in time to see a car pull up. When it stopped, the back door opened, and the man pushed Max inside.

Somehow she knew if Max got in, he was going on a one-way trip.

With no time for making plans, Annie did the only thing she could think of. Flying across the space that separated her from the car, she leveled a two-handed blow to the back of the man's neck. He grunted and fell to his side, giving her the opportunity to grab Max's arm and pull him out of the car.

Max gave her a startled look but recovered quickly. As they dashed toward the building and then along the wooden pier, a shot rang out, plowing into the siding inches from her head.

She and Max ducked around a corner, then along the back of the building. She had no idea where they were going, but she was sure that soon a whole squad of people would be looking for them.

The pier was closed off by a gated chain-link fence topped by razor wire. The gate was unlocked, and they dashed inside. But when they turned the corner, there was another fence and nowhere else to go.

"Now what?" Max growled as he rattled the metal and looked up at the wire she knew would slash their flesh.

Chapter Eleven

Annie's heart was beating so hard she thought it might pound its way through the wall of her chest.

Inside the enclosure, hugging the building, was a storage shed, the entrance illuminated by an overhead bulb.

Telling herself to stay calm, she ran to the shed and tried to open the door. The knob didn't budge, but she felt some kind of connection to the cold metal that she couldn't explain. She'd had the same feeling after Max had left her alone, handcuffed to the bed. Then she'd found a pin to stick into the lock. Now she hissed, "Give me your keys."

"What good is that going to do?"

"Just give them to me!"

Max cut her a sharp look, then reached into his pocket and pulled out a ring with several keys. Still fighting to stay steady, she selected one and tried to fit it into the lock. When it refused to go in, she found another that would slip into the mechanism. It felt as if there was a line of power between her fingers and the lock as she manipulated the key, jiggling it in a way she didn't really understand. It just felt right.

Grasping the knob with her other hand, she turned

and pushed. The door opened, just as she heard shouting somewhere behind them.

"Come on." Pulling the key from the knob, she slipped inside the storage shed. Max followed, gently closing and locking the door behind them.

The only light filtered in through cracks in the corners of the walls. As her eyes adjusted, she could see various furnishings from the club, including tables and chairs and several of the large wooden panels like the ones she'd seen covering the walls of the hallway.

Swiftly, Max moved the panels aside. "Back there," he whispered.

She ducked behind the wood, and Max followed, pulling the screens into place, then turning and folding her into his arms.

She came willingly, leaning against him in the darkness behind the panels. She'd managed to stay calm during the past few frantic moments; now she felt her knees buckle and had to grasp him to stay upright.

He held her in the confined space, running his hands up and down her back and moving his lips against her ear. His breath was warm against her skin, but his voice was barely audible as he said, "Thank you."

Her throat was too constricted to answer, and she could only nod. Probably he wanted to know how she'd opened the door. Would he believe her when she told him that she had simply sensed she could make a key work if she could fit it into the slot?

There was no point in worrying about what would happen later. They had to live through the here and now. Live through the manhunt outside.

Max did not speak again, which was prudent, considering that Nicki no doubt had a posse of men looking for them. Like when she and her mother and sister had been spotted near a tunnel entrance.

She tried to hang on to that thought. But it flitted away, as so many others had done.

When Max pulled her closer and nuzzled her hair, she melted against him. Probably, he was trying to take her mind off the people searching for them. People who would surely kill them.

She was so tired of questioning everything that happened between them. Closing her eyes, she rested her head on his shoulder.

They were in a dangerous situation, and his embrace was sheltering, comforting. Yet, as always when she was in his arms, it was impossible not to react to this man on a more physical level. On a sexual level.

She leaned into him, reveling in his every touch, every caress. She thought of nothing, letting herself drift, focusing only on the way he made her feel.

Angry voices outside their hiding place jerked her back to reality.

She felt Max go rigid as the sound of running feet stopped directly outside the shed.

"Where the hell are they?" a man asked.

"If they tried to climb over that fence and jumped into the water, they'd get cut up pretty bad. But maybe they'd do it if they were desperate."

"If they're cut up, maybe the sharks'll get them."

The callous words and the laugh that followed made Annie shudder.

There was a moment of silence when the pursuers were probably searching the area. Finally one of the voices said, "Maybe they're in the shed."

Her heart leaped into her throat, then expanded to block her windpipe as somebody rattled the knob.

"It's locked. They must have gone somewhere else."

"We've already got the whole place covered."

"Yeah, well, I want a look inside. Who's got the key?"

"Nicki."

"I'll guard the door. Somebody go get the key."

Annie's breath had solidified in her lungs. She wanted to ask Max what they were going to do now, but she understood that any noise she made might be fatal. There was no doubt in her mind that the man outside was holding a gun on their hiding place—in case they weren't already a shark's dinner. And when the door was opened, he'd search the shed and find them—even behind the flimsy wood panels.

Beside her, Max's whole body tensed, and she knew he was getting ready to fight. She wanted to turn to face the enemy, but she couldn't do that now without making a telltale noise.

Of course, it felt as if she had already given herself away. In the darkness of the shed, it sounded as if every breath she and Max took must be audible through the metal walls.

She didn't know how much time passed, perhaps a minute or perhaps a century.

"What took you so long?" the man who had stayed outside growled.

"I can't fly. I got back here as fast as I could."

In the next second, she heard the key slip into the lock.

Her nerves screamed as she waited to hear the door open and braced to put up a fight.

Instead of the lock turning, she heard a low curse.

Another voice said, "Let me try it."

Thirty endless seconds passed before the other guy

muttered in disgust, "The damn lock is broken. If we can't get in there, they can't, either."

"So widen the search. Maybe somehow they made it back to the boat."

"Yeah."

The footsteps receded into the distance, and she sagged against Max.

He lowered his mouth to her ear. "Don't move. It could be a trick."

She nodded against his shoulder.

They stayed where they were, jammed together for several more minutes. Eyes closed, she pressed her face against his chest. Finally, when everything remained quiet outside, he asked, "What happened?"

"You mean how did I open the lock and why couldn't they get in?" she whispered.

"Yeah. That."

"Don't know." She swallowed. "I mean, somehow I was pretty sure I could open the door. Like with those handcuffs, I just did it."

"I was thinking of that when I gave you the keys."

"But I didn't know the key would fail for them."

She heard his answer rumble in his chest. "Okay. Maybe we'd better find out if we can get out of here."

Despite the warm, close atmosphere in the shed, his words sent a shiver over her skin. She stood with her shoulders against the wall and her palms pressed against her sides as Max quietly moved the panels out of the way, then crept to the door. She couldn't see what he was doing, and she felt her throat close again as she heard him twist the knob.

To her vast relief, the door opened a crack, letting cooler air into the shed. In moments it closed again.

Max turned back to her, still pitching his voice low.

"We're not locked in, but we have to make a decision. There's a whole mob of people out there beating the bushes for us. It's dangerous to leave this shed. But when they don't find us, they could come back—and they could break the door down if it doesn't open."

She nodded into the darkness. They might be in serious trouble either way. After trying to think her way out of the trap, she said, "This nightclub is on a pier."

"Yeah. I assume that's why they're using it as a drug depot. They can bring the stuff in by water, and some of the distribution can be that way, too."

"They *did* bring it here. I heard Nicki and a man talking about it."

"Then maybe we can nail them. But not now. I suggest we go over the side and under the pilings," Max continued.

She shuddered.

"You can't swim?"

"I...I don't know. If I can open locks, I can probably stay afloat. But isn't the water poisonous?" she asked with a small gulp.

He tipped his head to the side, looking at her consideringly. "We were in the water a couple of days ago. This coastline connects to the channel where I pulled you out."

He was right, of course. She remembered that now. But the first things that had happened here were all a blur.

"It's not so clean close to the pier, I'll grant you, but we'll survive," Max was saying.

"Okay," she agreed, because she had to take his word for it. "When we get close to the shore, I'll get out of the water and find us a car."

"Finding the car is my job," he answered immediately. "I'll do it." Cautiously, he opened the door again and stepped out.

She stayed inside with her pulse pounding in her ears. By the time he opened the door and said, "All clear," she could hardly hear the words.

She ducked low, following his example as they crossed the wooden boards. When they were outside the fence again, he stepped over the edge of the pier, and she saw him climbing down a wooden ladder.

Gritting her teeth, she followed him as quickly as possible. On the bottom rung, she hesitated, but no choking fumes rose to greet her. So she let go and landed in cold water that splashed up around her shoulders.

When she found she couldn't touch the bottom, she had a moment of panic, then realized she knew what to do and began to tread water.

"You okay?" Max whispered.

"Yes," she answered, then sputtered as a salty wave slapped her in the face. She looked doubtfully at the pilings. In the moonlight she saw that the understructure of the pier was slick and slimy in some places and covered by barnacles in others. Plastic cups and other debris bobbed in the waves.

She followed Max toward the shore, trying to make as little noise as possible as she swam. After about ten meters, she found she could touch the bottom, and she was beginning to relax when voices from above made her stop.

"You find anything?" one man said.

"Nothing."

The first speaker cursed. "Nicki's gonna be pissed if they get away."

"That's Gordon's problem. He was the one who let the woman coldcock him."

"I wouldn't want to be in his shoes. He'll be lucky if he doesn't end up in the swamp like that Jamie Jacobson."

"Yeah, people who get in Nicki's way have a habit of disappearing."

Annie looked toward Max. Were they speaking the literal truth? Were they going to kill the guy she'd assaulted?

"What about the shipment? Is she gonna move it out?"

"I think she'll let things settle down first."

As they crouched against the side of the pier, Max put a steadying hand on Annie's arm, and she moved closer to him, once again silently thanking The Protectors that he was with her.

As if to counter the feeling of closeness, a scene flashed into her mind. She was sitting in a bare room with an angry-looking man who asked her rapid-fire questions and screamed at her when she gave the wrong answers.

Too bad she couldn't hear the questions.

Was he the one she'd called Angelo when she'd awoken from her dream?

The feel of Max's fingers tightening on her arm brought her back to the present.

"Annie?" he whispered.

She straightened. "We have to get out of here."

"Unfortunately, there's a little problem."

She looked toward the shore. In the moonlight, she could see two men scanning the parking lot with giant flashlights. She had hoped they weren't going to get any closer to the pier. But when the light swung to the water, she and Max both ducked behind the pilings and crouched under the boards.

She was glad the water was dark, because she did not want to take a good look at it.

They stayed where they were until the lights moved away from the water. But the men remained in the parking lot.

"Can we take them?" she asked.

"Probably, but they're not the only ones looking for us."

"What are we going to do?" She struggled to keep her voice as even as his.

"Swim farther along the coast, then go ashore."

Taking her cue from him, she slipped into the water and began quietly swimming in the direction the tide was moving.

She was about thirty feet from the pier when suddenly the light swept across the water, heading straight toward her. Looking wildly around, she caught sight of Max. He dived, and she did the same. Below the surface, she held her breath as long as she could. Kicking upward, she stuck her head out, gulped in air, then went down again when the light came sweeping back toward her.

She was totally disoriented now, unsure of which direction she had come from and where she should be going. Fighting panic, she stayed under until her lungs were near bursting, then came up, gasping for air.

She was farther from shore and she had no idea where Max was. Terror threatened to swallow her, but she clenched her fists and ordered herself to keep functioning. When she turned in a circle, she located the pier and struck out in the opposite direction, angling toward shore. By force of will, she kept herself from calling out to Max. Was he all right? Had something happened to him when he'd dived under the water?

She had no way of knowing, and she had to fight the sick feeling that rose in her throat. They had started off as enemies. At the beginning she had been sure that she had to get away from him. Now, unable to locate him, she could hardly cope with the emotions swirling through her.

She was so tired it was tempting to simply let herself float, even if she was in danger of being swept out to sea. But she hadn't reached that point yet, so she kept struggling toward shallow water. Finally, she could stand up again. Crouching low, she flopped to the wet sand. Ahead of her was a stretch of undeveloped land, covered with scrubby vegetation. She knew there might be snakes or even alligators lurking in the underbrush.

Hoping such creatures didn't come down to the beach, she rolled to her back and lay in her wet clothing, staring up at the stars, marveling at how bright and sharp they looked. Before, she had seen them only through a muddy filter. She wanted to think about that more, but instead, she pulled her mind back to the danger around her.

She probably wasn't far enough from the nightclub, and Nicki's men would be combing the beach looking for her.

She was exhausted. And wet. And she didn't know what the carp she was going to do.

They had sent her here to do a job, but they had no idea of the dangers she would face. They had doomed her to failure. She wanted to scream at them for being such fools—but she didn't even know who they were. And of course, she couldn't blame her present predicament on them. She'd asked to go with Max tonight because she'd wanted to help him. If she was honest, she'd admit she hadn't wanted to be separated from him, either. Well, they were separated now.

She wasn't sure how long she lay there before she heard a voice—low and urgent.

"Annie? Are you okay?"

"Max?" At first she thought she might have dreamed him because she wanted him to be with her so badly. Slowly, afraid that no one was really there, afraid she was having some sort of new mental disturbance, she turned her head—and saw him kneeling beside her on the sand. "Annie, are you hurt?"

He was there. He was really at her side. Gladness surged within her. Sitting up, she clasped him to her, unable to cope with the strength of her relief. "Max! I thought you were gone."

"Yeah. I had a couple of bad moments after we got separated. Then I spotted you on the beach." He sounded casual, but then he gave her a fierce hug. She wanted to cling to him, but knew they couldn't stay where they were.

When he eased away from her, she turned him loose.

"Come on," he urged.

"Where are we going?"

"Not back to the boat, that's for sure. They'll be looking for us there."

She felt too tired to move, but because she couldn't show him how weak and needy she was, she pushed herself to her feet. He clasped her hand, leading her away from the nightclub. Though she wanted to ask where they were going, she didn't waste the breath and simply followed him down the beach.

He led her to the water, and they walked where their footprints would wash away. They tromped past the wilderness area, then came out onto a lawn. To her right was an impossibly large white house that looked out over the water.

"This is an estate?" she murmured. "Where rich people live?" she murmured.

"Yeah."

They hurried across the lawn to a low wall. On the other side was another large house. The flamboyant structures loomed at regular intervals. She tried to imagine living in a place so large.

Max kept them moving rapidly past several boat docks where she could see various vessels moored.

Finally, he stopped under a large palm tree. "Stay here."

Earlier she might have objected; now she did as he asked. She watched him climb onto a dock and move at a crouch toward a large cabin cruiser. A lamp high on a pole illuminated the area, and her stomach clenched as he stepped into the circle of light, exposing himself to attack.

Swiftly he climbed onto the deck of the boat, then disappeared inside. As he vanished from view, her heart began to pound in her chest.

She hated hiding uselessly in the shadows. But there was nothing she could do to help him now. If she climbed onto the boat, he would think she was an attacker.

So she stood in her wet shirt and jeans, working to keep her teeth from chattering and straining her eyes into the darkness, but she couldn't see Max or anyone else.

Once again, it seemed as if hours passed before he reappeared on the deck and waved her forward. A glad cry rose in her throat, but she kept it locked inside as she ran across the lawn and scrambled up on the pier. When she got to the boat, Max reached for her arm, helping her onto the deck.

Feeling slightly dazed, she let him lead her into a large lounge, then downstairs and into a cabin.

She had thought *his* boat was luxurious. There was enough light coming in from the lamp out on the dock for her to see that this craft was larger and more opulent. The cabin into which he ushered her was rich with polished wood and leather.

"Is it all right to stay here?" she asked. "I think somebody will object."

"I'm betting they won't know about it." He gave a short laugh. "You remember when that guy, Andrew Cunanan, killed Versace? It turned out he'd been living on some rich dude's boat tied up behind his house."

She shook her head. She was beyond acting as if she understood references that had no meaning for her.

"Versace?"

He tipped his head to one side. "You don't remember that famous murder case?"

"I'm sorry…no." She sighed. "And I am tired of pretending."

He regarded her gravely, then shifted his weight from one foot to the other. "We should get you warm and dry."

She looked down at her clinging clothing, then back at him. His hair was plastered to his head, his shirt to his broad chest. "Not just me. You, too."

"Let's see what there is to wear." He opened a closet and began looking through clothing on hangers until he pulled out a terry-cloth robe. "Start with this. And let's hope that we can use the shower without turning on the generator.'' He opened the door to the head and looked inside. ''We'd better not switch on any lights.''

Reaching into the shower, he turned the taps. After a few moments, he said, ''I don't think we're going to get hot water.''

''That's okay.''

He swung back to her. ''You're used to cold showers?''

''I think so, yes,'' she answered. ''I think I am used to less than luxurious conditions.''

''I'll give you some privacy.''

When he left the cabin, she stepped into the bathroom and pulled off her wet clothes. In truth, the cold shower wasn't bad at all, since she was already cold and clammy.

Using the shampoo and soap she found on a shelf, she washed and rinsed her hair and body. Then, moving her hand slowly upward, she felt for the tattoo under her arm, wishing it had magically disappeared.

No such luck. It was still there, and she closed her eyes as she fingered the raised skin. The damn mark meant something, but she didn't know what. She wanted to scream out her frustration. Instead, she turned off the water with a jerky movement.

After drying herself, she went in search of Max and found him emerging from another cabin where he had obviously showered and found clean clothing.

He looked from her to the window and back again. ''I need to tell Light Street about the drugs—and about Jamie Jacobson.''

''Tell them? How?''

''I've got to find a phone. Mine didn't survive that swim.''

She clamped her hand over his shoulder. ''Not now!''

"Yes, now." He gathered her close, rubbing his hands in circles across her back. "I know you don't want to stay here alone, but I can move faster by myself."

"I can stay by myself!"

"Good." After a moment, he stepped away from her and started opening drawers. "I'd feel better if you had a weapon."

"You expect to find a gun—just like that?"

"You have no faith in the American reverence for defending home and hearth." As he spoke he strode into the companionway, then entered another stateroom. Again he searched through the drawers. In the third room, to her surprise, he did find a gun, a revolver. And the bullets were in a nearby box. "You know how to use this?" he asked.

She took the gun, checked and loaded it. "Yes."

"Then I'll be back as soon as I can."

Again she wanted to protest, but she quietly went back to the cabin where she'd showered and sat down in the chair in the corner, wondering if she was doomed to spend her life waiting for Max Dakota to come back. A swirl of emotions threatened to overwhelm her, but she held them in check, because she had to focus on keeping watch.

Twenty minutes later she sat up straighter when she felt the boat shift. Someone had stepped onto the deck, and was now coming rapidly down the stairs.

"Don't shoot!" Max called out. "It's me." He stepped into the room.

She stood. "You made the call."

"Piece of cake."

"Cake? What does cake have to do with it?"

He tipped his head to one side. "One of our strange English-language expressions."

"Don't tease me. Tell me what you did."

"There was a big cabana out by the pool. They had a phone inside. I made a quick call to my office. They'll alert the DEA—Drug Enforcement Administration."

She breathed out a little sigh. "Do we have to do anything?"

"We're out of it at the moment. Our best bet is to get some sleep."

"Okay," she answered, accepting his judgment.

His gaze bored into her, reminding her that she was naked under the robe.

"How are you holding up?" he asked.

"I've been better," she answered, because the simple explanation was easier than dealing with the emotions threatening to break through the wall she'd built up around them.

"There's something I need to say," he told her.

Her own worries faded into the background when she noticed the anger in his voice. "Something bad?"

"Yeah. I'm sorry things turned out the way they did. It looks like my informant who was taking my money turned us in to Nicki." His face contorted. "I've been running this operation on a kind of fast-and-loose basis. Too damn loose. It was lucky you insisted on coming along tonight, otherwise I'd probably be facedown in the swamp by now."

"No!"

"Of course, in the process of taking you to Nicki's place tonight, I almost got you killed, too."

His flat tone and the defeated look on his face sent her hurtling across the space between them so she could wrap her arms around him. He held himself stiffly for a moment, then leaned into her as a shuddering sigh escaped her lips.

"Max, don't blame yourself."

She curved her body as tightly to his as her robe and his clothing would permit. Frustrated by the fabric, she opened some of the buttons on the front of his shirt and slipped her hand inside.

His eyes were intense as he stared down at her. "Honey, I appreciate the sentiment, but you're, uh, being kind of provocative."

She raised her chin. Then truly astonished by her own boldness, she said, "I hope so."

When he continued to stare down at her, she added, "Max, I'm not going to throw myself at you. Well, not any further than this. I'm hoping you have enough sense to take over."

Then she waited with her heart pounding to see if he was going to turn away from what she offered.

Chapter Twelve

He didn't answer her with words. Instead, he lowered his mouth. As his lips touched hers, she made a sound that was part plea, part invitation.

Heat flared between them as he angled his head first one way, then the other.

"Annie." His warm breath caressed her mouth as he spoke. Then his lips were moving over hers with an urgency that sent a shock wave through her, making her feel as though the boat was rocking wildly under her feet, although she knew it was not.

Last time, he'd kissed her with passion. This time, she felt something more—a desperation that robbed her of breath. He needed her, and the realization was intoxicating.

Until now he had been so strong and in charge. Now he clung to her in a way that made her feel both weak and powerful.

The hand still inside his shirt began to move restlessly against his hot skin. Enjoying the sensation of crisp hair against her fingers, she opened more buttons and stroked the skin it laid bare. When she brushed the hard nubs of his nipples, he sucked in a strangled breath.

Anxiously, she lifted her head. "Does that hurt you?"

He looked down, his eyes warm as they met hers. "Does this?" he asked, slipping his hand inside her robe and stroking her tight nipples. She could only answer with a quick, indrawn breath.

He smiled, and she basked in the warmth of that smile. The only thought in her mind was that she needed to get closer to him—as close as possible. Seeking his heat and strength, she finished with the buttons of his shirt and pulled the fabric aside. But that wasn't enough.

Wondering how she'd become so bold, she began fumbling with the buckle of his belt. He helped her, opening the buckle, then unzipping his borrowed jeans and stepping out of them before tearing off the shirt he still wore.

In seconds, he was naked, his body hard and tense—and fascinating. She found the sides of his hips, then moved one hand inward, finding his sex. It was large and hard, and standing out from his body as though it had a life of its own.

She was drawn to that part of him. Once again astonished at herself, she trailed her fingers over the rigid shaft, marveling at the silky feel of his skin and the hardness beneath.

Enthralled, she stroked him, then clasped him in a tight embrace. He dragged in a shuddering breath, but this time she knew she wasn't hurting him.

Still, his hand closed over her wrist. "Honey, if you don't want this to be over before it starts, you'd better find some other focus for that very sexy hand of yours."

She didn't quite follow what he was saying. But she guessed that her touch might be too intense. So she inched her hand upward, then pressed her palm against his flat belly, feeling his muscles jump.

"My turn," he whispered, tugging at the belt of her robe, pulling it out of the way, then spreading the front open. But he didn't stop there. In one quick motion, he swept the heavy garment from her shoulders. The weight dragged it downward, and suddenly her arms were trapped. She felt a spurt of panic as she tried to move them. Then she heard him draw in a breath, and her nerves jumped again as she looked up at him.

"You are so beautiful," he said.

"Am I?" she asked, because she couldn't believe the simple words.

"Oh, yes." He caressed her breasts, bringing the already tight crests to points of pure sensation. And when he gently stroked them, then rolled them between his thumbs and fingers, he wrung another gasp of pleasure from her.

When he folded her into his arms, the shock of that intimate contact made her head spin.

He gathered her more tightly to himself and lowered his head for a deep, sweet kiss. As he did, the whirlwind of emotion she felt threatened her balance. She struggled to stay on her feet when he led her across the room toward the double bed attached to one bulkhead.

She knew she wanted to be with him like this. At the same time, now that they were standing beside the bed—both naked—some deeply buried taboos made her throat close. Even if she didn't want to admit it, she knew this was wrong. Uncertainty leaped inside her.

He must have sensed her change of mood, because he lifted his head and said, "Annie?"

She couldn't speak. All she could do was stand there, clenching and unclenching one fist.

His hands dropped away from her body. "This time, were you trying to forget about the thugs looking for us?" he asked, his voice gritty.

"No. I was thinking only about being with you."

He sighed. "Annie, you don't have to do anything you don't want to."

"Max." She knew he couldn't understand the uncertainties swirling within her. She didn't entirely understand them herself. But she knew that in Hermosa Harbor, Florida, people did what they wanted, when they wanted. And she wasn't like them.

She looked at him, seeing regret and pain in his eyes.

"Max," she said again, reaching for him, clinging to him. She dragged in a shuddering breath, then let it out in a rush. When she'd accused him of being intimate with Nicki, she had spoken of sexual intercourse. Now she used another term, a forbidden term. "I wanted to…make love with you. But then we were both naked and I looked at the bed, and something inside me told me that what we were doing was wrong."

He tipped her head up, looking down into her worried face. "Morality rearing its ugly head again?"

"Unfortunately, yes!" She struggled to rein in her frustration and to find the right words. "But I want to be with you."

"Why?"

She was terrified that he would pull away from her, and she knew she had to say something. So she blurted out the truth—as much of the truth as she knew. "Because it feels good. More than just physically good. You touch something deep inside me…." Her voice trailed off, and she heaved a sigh. "I think it's because I have never met a man I care about as much as you."

"You've only known me for a few days."

"A few very intense days," she countered. It was so unreal to be here with him like this. It was forbidden. Yet...

He didn't speak, and she knew she had to fill the silence with words he would believe. Even when he had believed so little of what she had told him.

"Max, most of my memories before Hermosa Harbor are gone. But I think I haven't had much happiness in my life. Being with you makes something inside me...unfurl."

Again words failed her. She wasn't saying what she meant, so she ended the short speech by clasping her hands around the back of his head, bringing his mouth back to hers for a kiss that flared hot and fierce between them. Desperate to keep him from leaving her now, she pulled him down to the bed.

When he lifted his head, they were side by side and both breathing hard. But she knew she hadn't won yet when he said, "This may be all wrong for you."

"I don't think so."

Levering himself up on one elbow, he gently stroked her lips with his finger. "Annie, I've thought from the first that you weren't very experienced with men."

"Does that matter to you?" she asked.

His hand continued to stroke her face, her hair. "Maybe I'd better ask a different question. Do you, um, know what making love means?"

She felt heat flood her face, but she was not going to look away from him. "You mean physically?"

He kept his gaze steady on her. "Yeah."

She swallowed, realizing she hadn't really thought about what she'd been planning to do with him. Not exactly. She had only wanted to be close to him. As close as a woman could be to a man. Now a more ex-

plicit picture leaped into her mind—one that made her
face grow hot. The words were too hard to say, so she
reached between them, touching the part of him that she
had already clasped. It had been large and hard. Now it
was softer, less formidable. "You put this...inside me."

"Where?" he asked.

She wanted to duck away from him, but she was
afraid that if she didn't answer, he would climb out of
the bed.

"Down here." She took his hand, carrying it to the
place that throbbed with heat when he kissed her and
caressed her.

He moved his hand away from that place, then
reached to pull at the sheet and coverlet they were lying
on top of. "Contrary to what you may think, I find
having this conversation buck naked a little disconcert-
ing. Raise your hips so we can get under the covers."

She was glad to do as he asked. After they were
settled again, he reached for her hand and knit his fingers with hers. When he spoke, his voice was gritty.
"Annie, I think you are very sweet and very naive. Not
like any woman I've ever met. And I also think we can't
go any further, not if that's all you know about it."

"It's not all I know!"

"Okay, what else?"

"I know how you make me feel when you kiss me,
when you touch me."

She saw his Adam's apple bob. "Yeah, but that
doesn't mean I wouldn't be taking advantage of you.
And now that we're talking about it calmly, I've got a
little better handle on responsible behavior. I'm not going to take a chance on getting you pregnant. Because,
in case you don't remember, making love is the way
people make babies."

"Oh," she answered, feeling stupid. Had she known that? It sounded right, now that he'd told her.

She pressed the back of her head into the pillow, staring up at the ceiling, once again fighting to hold back the tears that burned behind her eyes. She had been carried along by emotions. Consequences had not even entered her mind. Beside her, she heard Max curse.

"Come here," he said gruffly. Rolling toward her, he clasped her in his arms again.

She curled against him, clung to him—this time for comfort as much as for anything else.

"Annie, Annie," he murmured. "You are such a mystery. So lost and yet so strong. You don't hesitate to go up against an armed man, but making love frightens you even if you won't admit that to me."

She nodded slightly. "I guess that's right."

"Where the hell do you come from?"

"If I could answer that question, I would."

"I know," he said with quiet conviction.

"You do?"

"Yeah, I do. After what we've been through together tonight, I trust you with my life."

"Oh, Max."

She twined her arms around his body, holding tight.

He cradled her against him, then began speaking again. "You've lost your memory, but that's not the only thing that's different about you."

"What else?"

"The way you react to this culture is wildly different from someone who was born here."

"I know," she murmured, thinking about the way she talked and about the nightclub, remembering the people she'd seen practically having sexual intercourse in the hallway. And the others at the tables and on the dance floor, shamelessly kissing. "I keep trying to pretend that I'm like everyone else, but it takes a lot of energy."

He laughed and stroked her shoulder. "Sometimes it seems like you're from another century."

His words sent a small shiver over her skin. "What century?" she asked.

"I don't know. Some time in the past, when women were expected to be virgins until they married. The only problem with that theory is that you told me you can drive a car."

She glimpsed a memory. "Yes. An automatic. Not a stick shift. And I can start the engine with a wire."

"A valuable talent in some circles."

Her smile was fleeting. "But it's hard for me to talk about sex."

"I can see that."

"With you…it feels okay. Well, not okay, exactly. But I have to discuss it if I'm going to make you stop backing away from me." She raised her eyes to his. "Are you looking for excuses to go sleep in another bed?"

He released the lock of her hair he'd been twining around her fingers and brushed her lips with his, then he slid his mouth to her ear, taking her lobe between his teeth and playing with it. Everything he did brought back the wonderful hot feelings he had kindled in her before.

"Max, please…" she breathed, hating the pleading sound of her voice. Looking down at the covers over his hips, she saw that he had changed again. She was pretty sure the male part of him she craved was once again hard.

The physical change in him gave her hope that he

wasn't going to climb out of the bed and leave her alone.

It was his words that dashed her hopes. "We can't make love," he said in a thick voice.

"Don't tell me that!"

"But we can do other things."

She couldn't ask what he meant. She could only lower her head, her mouth raining wet kisses on his shoulder.

He ran his fingers through her hair and trailed his other hand down her back to her bottom, pressing her center against his hip.

Heat curled through her like hot butterscotch syrup. Thinking that everything might be all right, after all, she brought her mouth up to his so that they could exchange openmouthed kisses that slowly became deeper, more intimate.

He moved his hands up and down her sides, sliding them over her ribs, her hips, her thighs, making her skin feel hot and prickly—not just where he touched, but everywhere. Especially that place hidden between her legs—that place that had begun to ache again.

Taking her by surprise, he rolled her onto her back and leaned over her, bringing his mouth to her breast, circling his tongue around the taut crest, then sucking it into his mouth. The wet heat and the tugging pressure made her cry out.

"Max, I feel like I'm going to explode," she gasped.

"That's the idea."

She couldn't follow his logic, not when her brain was shutting down. Her hands clamped his shoulders, because she needed to hang on to him.

"Annie, you are so sexy," he murmured as his fingers slid between her legs and found the moist heat where her body begged for his touch.

He stroked her there, and she almost forgot to breathe as she arched into the caress. Without conscious thought, she moved her hips, rubbing herself against his fingers, desperate for what only this man could give her.

"Oh, Max." The feelings he was creating overwhelmed her. He caressed her with his long fingers, dipping inside her, pressing against her.

Before, she had told him she was about to explode. It was nothing compared to what she felt now as one of his hands moved between her legs and the other played with one of her aching nipples. The touch of those two hands built her need for something just beyond her grasp, carried her up and up to a place she had never known existed.

"Keep doing that," she gasped, hardly knowing she had spoken aloud. "Keep doing it!"

He stayed with her, kissing her cheek and her hair as she came undone in a burst of pleasure that racked her whole body.

She drifted back to herself, still in his arms. Looking at him in wonder, she was hardly able to believe the feelings that swept over her, that still came to her in little clenching waves.

"Thank you," she gasped, knowing words were inadequate. All the stress was gone from her now, and it was tempting to close her eyes and drift off to sleep. But she felt the tension in his body, and she was pretty sure he hadn't experienced the same pleasure she had.

"You should feel that, too, shouldn't you?" she whispered.

"You don't have to worry about me," he said, the words brittle.

"Maybe not. But I want to," she answered, then reached under the covers and found him. "Tell me how to make you feel that explosion go off in your body," she demanded, although he had already given her clues.

He lay back, his breath coming hard and fast. Then he closed his hand around hers.

"This way," he said in a strangled voice as he showed her what to do.

She did as he asked, watching his face, listening to the sound of his harsh breathing, thrilling to the way he responded to her. And when his body jerked and he cried out in pleasure, she felt tears gather in her eyes. Tears of joy, but joy mixed with sadness, because she wanted so much more with this man. But she was afraid this was all they would ever have together.

SHERIFF BERT TRAINER'S Glock was drawn as he pulled *The Wrong Stuff* against the dock with his free hand. When he climbed onto the boat the deck shifted under his weight. He crouched low, heading toward the interior of the cabin cruiser. It was a nice boat, he thought. Not the most luxurious, but a comfortable place to live.

Truthfully, he didn't expect to find Max Dakota and his girlfriend here. Dakota wasn't going to take the chance of getting caught flat-footed, not when the other side had declared war. But it was clear the guy had fully intended to come back here tonight—he hadn't had a chance to tidy up.

The sheriff made a quick sweep of the boat, satisfying himself that he was the only one on board. Then he began searching the drawers in the main living area.

When he didn't find anything interesting, he proceeded below again and began looking through the two cabins. In the smaller one, he found a bunch of bags from a cheap department store and new woman's clothing neatly folded on the bed. It looked as if Max had bought his girlfriend a whole wardrobe. Too bad she'd had to leave it behind.

The computer was also a nice find. An expensive little laptop. He could take that with him and work on it at his leisure. But he was still interested in what else he might find.

He hit pay dirt when he found some papers stuffed into a drawer. Not in Dakota's handwriting—he knew that well enough. He presumed it was the woman, Annie Oakland, who had put down a bunch of facts about Sea Kingdom.

Then he found another piece of paper with a symbol on it. An X in a circle.

He felt as though he'd suddenly stepped out of the warm Florida night into an arctic wasteland.

No. It couldn't be. But when he blinked, it didn't go away.

He'd been waiting for years to see the damn thing. Waiting and hoping against hope it wouldn't happen. And now here it was.

IT SEEMED to Annie as if she had only a few minutes to snuggle in Max's arms. Then he stirred beside her, and she sensed that he was getting ready to climb out of bed. To keep him with her, she circled his wrist with her hand.

In response, he brushed her cheek with his lips. "I'd love to hold you naked in bed while we both get some sleep, but I don't think it's such a great idea. We need to put some clothes on. And one of us needs to keep guard."

"I can do it."

"Later. I'll take the first shift."

"Okay."

For a while she'd forgotten about the armed men out there looking for them. Now she realized it was possible that the men from the club could find their hiding place. So she pulled on a man's shirt and shorts she found in the dresser.

Max climbed out of bed and dressed in the borrowed clothing he'd been wearing, taking the gun with him.

Some time later he came back. Outside, the sun was up, and she knew he hadn't woken her to do guard duty.

He put the gun on the dresser again and laid an armload of clothes on the bed.

"You should have let me take a turn," she said.

"You needed the sleep. You had quite an eventful night."

"So did you," she answered as she poked through the clothing. It wasn't much like what she'd borrowed from Max or what they'd bought for her the day before. Everything here was gaudy, as though the woman who wore them wanted to call attention to herself.

She glanced up to see Max leaning against the dresser, watching her.

"Not your taste?" he asked.

She wrinkled her nose. Still, she didn't want to wear men's clothing when she left the boat, so she pulled on a pair of white shorts that fit pretty well. She had just pulled on a knit shirt with glitter studded across the front when a voice growled, "Put your hands above your head, and don't move."

Chapter Thirteen

Hands above his head, Max turned to face the doorway.
The man standing there was wearing the uniform of a
security company and looked like a bouncer a little past
his prime. But the gun in his hand argued for cooper-
ation, especially since Annie was standing in the room.

"What the hell are you doing making yourself at
home on Mr. Perkins's boat?" the man asked. "This is
private property. But I'm sure you know that already."

Max relaxed a fraction. He'd taken a calculated risk
last night when they'd needed a place to hide. Apparently this guy was conscientious about patrolling his
boss's property. But at least he wasn't one of the thugs
from Nicki's Paradise.

Never taking his gaze off the gun, Max said, "I'm a
special agent investigating a murder. Last night my partner and I were chased by drug dealers who have been
operating in Hermosa Harbor like they own the place.
We took refuge in this boat because it was a safe place
to stay."

The security guard snorted. "So you say."

"You can call my agency and get confirmation,"
Max said, keeping his focus on the man with the gun,
but trying to look at Annie from the corner of his eye.

She'd acted rashly before. If she pulled some stunt now, she could get them both killed.

The man still looked doubtful. "Yeah, sure, I can call the number you give me. But how do I know it's not just your low-life friends on the other end of the line? I think the better choice is to call Sheriff Trainer."

Great, Max thought, but he kept his voice even. "Trainer doesn't know about my assignment. I've been working undercover."

"Uh-huh. Maybe he knows you're one of the drug dealers. Why don't I just turn you over to him?"

Max remained impassive—because his life and Annie's depended on his keeping his cool. "That would be counterproductive," he said.

"I have a responsibility to Mr. Perkins. When he comes home tonight…" The guy's voice trailed off, as though he realized he'd just given away information.

"I'm sure he'll be pleased with your excellent performance," Max said.

From the corner of his eye, he could see Annie's body tense. But the security guard's total focus was on him; probably he didn't consider a woman too much of a threat.

Annie moved, taking the guard totally by surprise.

Max had time to curse as she brought the guy down. The gun went flying. Max kicked it under the dresser, then turned to the struggling figures. Annie had hauled the guard up onto the bed.

"Don't kill him!" Max shouted. "He's just doing his job."

"I won't hurt him," Annie said puffing. She was already using a bra to tie the guard's hands behind his back.

Max grabbed the gun she'd left on the dresser. Pointing it at the guard, he said, "Settle down."

"Get her off me!"

"Are his hands secure?" he asked Annie.

"Yes."

Training the revolver on the men, Max moved closer. "Tie his legs," he told her.

Annie looked around, grabbed a pair of panty hose and finished the job.

Max checked the bonds, then quickly searched the guard's pockets, from which he extracted a set of keys. After unclipping the man's cell phone from his belt, he lifted the captive into the chair and tied him to it.

"I'm sorry you're caught in the middle of a bad situation," Max said. "We'll call the Perkins house tonight and get someone to free you."

"I'll get you for this!"

"I hope not."

Max fixed a gag over the man's mouth, then stuck the gun into his own belt and covered it with his shirt. Turning to Annie, he said, "We'd better split."

"You mean get out of here?"

"Exactly."

ANNIE LOOKED BACK at the guard. "I'm sorry," she murmured. When the man glared at her, she followed Max out of the room.

Outside, the sun was shining, and a gentle breeze was blowing off the water.

"Just act like we belong here," he said, seeming to enjoy a morning stroll as he led her away from the ocean. He was good at this, she thought. He knew how to play a lot of roles; he knew when to talk to people and when to fight. He had said someone had trained her for a secret mission. Well, his training was better than hers.

She saw the cabana where he must have made the phone call the night before. At the main house, he stopped beside a black SUV. After trying several of the guard's keys, he found one that fit the lock.

They both got in and he headed up a driveway. When he reached the road, he sighed. "Max Dakota strikes again."

"What do you mean?"

"I mean, that boat wasn't such a great place to hide out."

"It would have been, if that guard hadn't been so conscientious. So let's put it behind us," she said.

After a moment, he gave a tight nod. "Okay," he answered in a low voice, then added, "I think what we need to do now is get the hell out of Florida."

She felt panic grab her. "No!"

His head whipped toward her. "Why not?"

"I...I can't go. I have to get to Sea Kingdom. And first I have to leave that piece of paper at Fort De Leon. I haven't even done that yet."

Max shook his head. "We're going to be a lot safer somewhere else. Our fingerprints are all over that boat. That may not be a problem for you since yours aren't on record, but mine are in the FBI database."

"You can leave," she said, "but I have to stay here."

"I'm not going without you."

"You don't owe me anything," she said, making an effort to speak calmly and directly.

He cast her an annoyed glance. "I don't much like your attitude."

"Why not?"

"Because I thought the two of us had gotten close last night. At least, I felt that way after you let me touch you where I'm pretty sure no one else has."

She swallowed hard. "Oh, Max, I..." That was all she said before stopping and scrambling for words. There was so much she wanted to say to this man, but she didn't know how to say it. Or even if she should. Reaching over, she laid her hand over his.

Max pulled to the curb in the residential neighborhood, under a tree covered with pink flowers. The blossoms and their scent surrounded the car, lending an air of unreality as he cut the engine and reached for her. Without hesitation, she came into his arms, clinging to him, feeling herself shake.

Hardly able to get the words out, she whispered, "Sometimes I...I feel like I'm not...acting on my own. Like *something* is making me do what I'm doing. Like when you said we should leave Florida, I knew I couldn't do it."

The admission was like jumping off the top of a tall building. She clung to Max, fighting the hot feeling in the back of her throat.

"Annie, we have to do something about you," he said in a tight voice.

She raised her head and stared at him. "What?"

"Get rid of that thing under your skin."

She felt a shudder go through her. "I can't."

"Are you afraid it will hurt?"

"No." She moistened lips that had suddenly turned dry as sand. "It's part of me."

"Yeah."

"How does that make you feel about me?" she managed.

He ran his fingers through her hair. "I'm okay with

it,'' he said, and she wondered if he was telling the truth. Before she could ask any more questions, he changed the subject. ''What we have to do is get ourselves some new transportation. Then we have to tell someone that security guard is on the boat.''

''Yes.''

''And we have to make sure Trainer doesn't scoop us up.''

''Right,'' she agreed, feeling her throat clog again. What he had said at the beginning of the conversation was correct. They should get out of Florida. But she knew that if she tried to do so, she'd die or go crazy or something equally horrible. So she'd just have to let Max take what precautions he could.

He drove to the outskirts of the business district to a place where he told her he could rent a car. After leaving her and the SUV several blocks away, he hurried to make the transaction, and she scooted down low in her seat, hoping Sheriff Trainer wouldn't walk by while she waited.

In less than twenty minutes, they were on the road again. Max checked them into a big motel on the highway, using a credit card under a different name.

When he'd closed the door to the room behind them, he said, ''If we're going to hang around here, we have to change our appearance.''

''Max, I know I'm putting us at risk.'' She should tell him again to just leave her. But the words wouldn't come.

He plowed on as though she hadn't spoken. ''I'm going out to buy some hair dye and scissors. And different clothing. You lock the door, and don't open it to anyone but me. And try to get some sleep. I'll be back as soon as I can.''

She nodded and he left. After locking the door behind him, she pulled the bedspread aside and lay down, her tension making it impossible to sleep. He was gone longer than she'd anticipated, and she was huddling on the bed with her stomach in knots and her heart pounding when finally, she heard a knock at the door.

Jumping up, she crossed the room and asked, "Who is it?"

"Max."

Quickly she turned the lock, and he stepped inside, closing the door behind him.

She was profoundly glad that he had come back to her safe and sound, but she'd learned to read his expression, and something on his face made her go tense. There was a look in his eyes that she'd seen before. The look that said he didn't trust her.

"Max?"

Wordlessly, he reached for her, and she felt a spurt of panic.

"It's okay," he said.

Still uncertain, she put up a defensive hand. When he pulled the hand down, real fear crackled through her. She'd given him her trust. Now she knew that that had been a serious mistake. She had been ordered to trust no one and she was finding out why.

In panic, she tried to jerk away. But he held her fast, then withdrew something from his pocket and put it over her face.

A muffled scream rose in her throat.

"Easy. Take it easy. I don't want to hurt you." His voice was like the buzz of insects in her ear. "Annie, I'm sorry." She was still trying to fight him when consciousness slipped from her.

EVEN THOUGH HER BRAIN felt as if it was mired in a fog, she registered panic because she didn't know where she was or what had happened. Then she forced her eyes open and was assailed by a red-hot pain under her arm.

The panic didn't lessen when she saw Max sitting beside her on the bed, staring down at her, his expression anxious and apologetic.

A recent memory leaped into her mind. Max had come back to the motel room. Then he had grabbed her. Hurt her. No. Not hurt, she corrected.

She should run from him. She tried to push herself up, but her body felt like lead. "What...what did you do to me?" she asked.

"You had a little operation. How do you feel?" he asked in a soft voice.

"An operation?" she gasped, cringing from him.

Regret flashed across his face. "I'm sorry I couldn't tell you about it first. But you said you wouldn't let me do anything about that damn implant. I knew I had to get it out of you. And I knew I had to make you unconscious to do it."

She stared at him, trying to take his words in, but her mind was too fuzzy for coherent thought.

He reached for her hand, held it gently. "It's gone. Do you feel different? Or have I made a serious mistake?"

She tried to consider the question, but she still didn't feel as if her mind and body belonged together.

"Annie?"

Closing her eyes, she struggled to collect her scattered thoughts. She was still missing a lot of her memories, and that was no less disturbing than it had been earlier. But something *was* different. She felt a new kind of calm that had been impossible before.

"I feel better," she murmured.

"Good, that's good. Can you tell me *how* it's better?"

"I don't feel like...I'm always in overdrive." She gave a small laugh. "But maybe that's because you gave me something to put me to sleep."

His hand clasped hers. "What if I told you I had us booked on a flight out of Florida? Would that send you into a panic like it did this morning?"

She focused on the idea of getting out of the area. "No," she finally said, knowing that something had truly changed within her.

"Do you want me to leave you alone?" he asked, and she saw the tension on his face. He had tricked her. But now she understood his motives. He had wanted to help her, and he had known she wouldn't allow it.

"Stay with me," she murmured.

He let out the breath he must have been holding. Shifting his grip on her hand, he meshed his fingers with hers.

She liked the feeling of being linked to him. Hand to hand.

"Can you lie down?" she asked. "I want to feel your body next to mine. Both of us naked," she added, because she didn't seem to be able to control her tongue.

"Naked." He laughed. "You're not going to get much rest if we're naked." He eased down beside her. "If the place where I cut you hurts too much, tell me. I can give you something for the pain."

"You operated here?"

"Uh-huh."

"Where did you get supplies?" she asked, stretching her coherence to its limits.

"My agency has contacts all over the country—well, all over the world. I called a doctor we've worked with. He's getting a large payment for giving me the stuff I needed."

"And you're trained in emergency medicine," she said. It wasn't a question.

"Yeah." He looked at her consideringly. "Maybe I gave you too much Mickey Mouse tingle juice."

"What?"

"Anesthetic. That's what they called it when I had my tonsils out as a kid."

"Tonsils?"

"Glands in my throat. They were sore all the time."

"Umm."

He didn't say anything else. But she wanted him to keep talking. "I love hearing about when you were a boy. About your family. You lived with your mother and father in a house?"

"Yeah."

"Did you have your own bedroom?"

"I had to share a bedroom with my brother."

"Tell me more things."

"Like what?"

"Everything."

"There was that time I got caught smoking behind the garage and my dad took me to a VA hospital to see guys with lung cancer."

"More," she demanded, not following all of it, but still fascinated.

"You want to hear about how I got sick in the pie-eating contest at the state fair?"

"Yes."

"I threw up a lot of cherry pie."

She laughed.

"How about in first grade when Ken Wilkie and I stopped up the sink in the boys' room?"

"Tell me good things."

"Like when my dad built us a tree house and let us spend the night in it?"

"Yes." She drifted on the sound of his voice, trying to stay awake. But finally she couldn't hold on to consciousness any longer.

Sometime later, her eyes snapped open. "Do you have...the thing you took out of me?" At his nod, she said, "I want to see it."

Without any objection, he got up from the bed, crossed to the dresser and picked up a small plastic bag. Carrying it back, he held it up.

It didn't look like much, just a flat rectangle with rounded corners. She murmured incoherently and drifted off to sleep.

She woke again some time later to hear Max talking on the phone in a low voice, and she had the feeling this had happened before.

"Yes. Good," he said, then looked over at her. "She's awake again. I'll talk to you later."

"Who was that?" she asked.

Crossing to the bed, he sat down again. "Steve Claiborne from my organization. He had some good news. The DEA got the drugs—and Nicki Armstrong. And one of her thugs is willing to cut a deal on the Jamie Jacobson murder."

"Cut a deal?"

"He's willing to confess to his part of it in exchange for a lighter sentence. So I don't have to leave with my assignment unfinished."

"Good," she murmured. "And Sheriff Trainer?"

"He's disappeared, but they'll find him," Max said soothingly.

He gently stroked her cheek. "How are you feeling?"

She moved her arm. "A little sore."

"Probably more than a little. What about some pain medication?"

"I can handle it."

His gaze locked on her. "Because you're tough?"

"Because I want to stay coherent."

He nodded. "Well, is there anything more you can tell me about yourself?"

She managed a small laugh. "You mean, was that thing screwing up my memories, and now I can tell you why I'm here?"

"Yeah."

She tried to concentrate on her past, but to no avail. "Sorry," she said. "I don't have any more insight."

"But you're willing to let me take you out of Florida?" he asked, and she wondered if he'd covered that ground before.

"Yes."

"And we can forget about leaving anything at the fort?"

She considered the question, then answered in the affirmative again.

"Good. Because Steve Claiborne is already on his way down here. He and another colleague, Jed Prentiss, are picking us up in a couple of hours."

"But we can come back before the governor goes to Sea Kingdom?" she asked anxiously, although the strength of the feeling had lessened. "Because even with that thing gone, I know I have to be there."

"We can."

"Should I trust you?"

"Yes."

"Like I did when you came through the door and slapped some kind of buzz-brain stuff over my face?" She couldn't stop the words from coming.

"Buzz-brain?"

"You know what I mean."

"Yeah." He looked apologetic. "I'm sorry. But it had to be done and you wouldn't let me."

"I understand," she whispered, then closed her eyes again, snuggling against him, thinking that they were alone in a bed and she'd like to make love with him. Instead, she went back to sleep.

The gentle stroking of Max's fingers in her hair woke her. "Time to get ready."

"Okay."

She lay there for a few minutes, then eased off the bed, wincing.

He was instantly at her side. "Now you're going to take something for the pain. When we get to Baltimore, Thorn Devereaux—I work with him, too—will give you a salve that will work better."

She dutifully swallowed two pills, then let Max help her on with her shoes and escort her to the car.

The medication not only took the edge off the pain, it made her drowsy again.

"Just go back to sleep," Max advised. "I'll take care of you."

Surrendering to the feeling, she closed her eyes. Her peaceful dreams lulled her into a deep sleep and she drifted off.

A sudden vibration and a deep rumble woke her with

a start. Her heart pounding, she looked around wildly and felt terror grip her throat. Where was she?

A narrow enclosure. A window.

She turned her head to the side and looked out. When she saw clouds and blue sky, she had to fight to drag in a breath. It came out again on a scream.

Sheer, blind panic tore at her.

She was up in the air again. High over the land. Last time, she had been terrified as she'd fallen…fallen….

This time was worse, because she was higher. Safety was farther from her grasp. And she knew she was going to die.

Chapter Fourteen

"Annie, it's all right." Max was beside her, gripping her.

She didn't listen. She couldn't listen.

Instead, she clawed at the belt holding her down. When the buckle released, she surged up.

In front of Max, she could see the back of another man sitting in a chair. There were windows in front of him and more terrifying open space. Banks of instruments surrounded him.

Was he the one who had trapped her here? Or was it someone named Angelo?

She struggled toward the enemy, but she was weak from what Max had given her.

"What the hell's going on?" the man demanded, looking over his shoulder.

"Everything's under control," Max called out.

But that was another of his easy lies. She had to get away. He had tricked her again, turned her over to this captor. She had to get down to the ground before she stopped breathing. She had to make the man in the front of the plane stop doing this to her.

Her hands were claws as she tore at Max's clothing, at his flesh.

He grunted, but she ignored him.

Struggling forward, she tried to reach the man in front. When she lunged at him, the surface under her feet lurched. Down. The plane was going down. Good. She had to get down. She heard someone curse, felt hands on her. But she fought with the strength of desperation.

Then someone pulled her from behind, pulled her back into the seat where she'd been sitting. Something covered her mouth and nose, and she had time for one more scream before the world swirled away.

"SHE IS ONE HELL of a fighter," a man's voice intoned.

"Yeah."

"I'm sorry. Did I give her too much? Is she okay?" the same unfamiliar voice asked urgently.

Annie's eyes fluttered open, and she focused on Max, then zinged to a blond man looming over her.

"Annie, are you all right? Annie?" Max demanded, and she thought he might have said the same thing earlier.

She tried to keep her eyes on Max. "I…"

"Jed here gave you a little more anesthetic. It was still in the kit. What happened to you?" he asked urgently. "I thought taking that thing out would solve the problem. I guess I was wrong."

She swallowed, then struggled to explain. "It's not about the thing from under my arm. We…we were so high. Above the ground. Like before." Her head swung to the side, but now her view of the outside was blocked. She knew they were still in the air, but she didn't have to look down, and that made the fear almost bearable.

"Like when you were in the sky over the bridge?" Max asked gently.

"Yes," she answered with a sobbing breath, because she realized it was true. She had been in something high in the sky. Then she had been falling…falling….

"You were scared then."

"Yes." Her hand closed around the seat arm in a death grip.

"But this is different. You're safe. You're with me, and I will *never* let anything bad happen to you. *Never again.*"

She knew in her heart that he meant those words, and hearing him say them made gladness leap inside her. She also knew he might not be able to keep the promise.

He sat beside her, gathered her to him. "We're in an airplane. We're going down soon."

She nodded, staying with him, trying to keep calm.

"This is Jed Prentiss." He nodded to the blond man next to him. "And that's Steve Claiborne flying this rig. They're the colleagues I told you about."

"I remember," was all she could manage.

"Go back to sleep," Max murmured, stroking her hair.

She clung to him, feeling her heart rate slowing. Her eyelids fluttered closed, and her fear drifted away. Not far away, but enough.

She didn't know how much later a change in the feel of the plane made her eyes jerk open. Then there was a bump, and she knew they were mercifully on the ground.

"Where are we?" she asked.

"Western Maryland. At a small private airport."

She looked toward the front of the plane, where Jed now sat with Steve.

"I could have killed us," she whispered to Max.

"You didn't. We're fine."

"But I feel so stupid," she blurted. "Your friends must think I'm crazy."

Steve must have heard her, because he turned around and laughed before saying, "Annie, all of us are stray dogs here. You're going to fit right in."

She didn't think it was true, but she clung to his words. As soon as the plane had stopped, men and women came out of a building with a curved roof. Steve cut the engine and opened the door, then lowered a short flight of steps.

Max climbed out, and she watched him shake hands with the men and hug the women. When she hung back, he reached toward her and helped her down the steps.

"And this is Annie Oakland. She's got all the right training to join our high-tech spy squad. But she had a little surgery this morning, so she's a bit shaky on her feet."

He curved his arm protectively around her. "Annie, this is Jason Zacharias, Kathryn Kelley, Thorn Devereaux and his wife, Cassie."

Annie struggled to sort them out. Jason was as tough-looking as the pilot and copilot. Kathryn was a redhead—but appeared much more sympathetic than Nicki Armstrong. A competent-looking blonde, Cassie stood next to her tall, good-looking husband, Thorn.

They all seemed friendly, but she felt overwhelmed, thinking that Max had probably been talking on the phone to them about her while she'd been sleeping.

And were Steve and Jed going to tell everyone what she'd done? Probably not in front of her.

Thorn stepped forward and handed her a small jar.

"Put this on the wound. The salve will heal it very quickly."

"Thank you," she murmured.

After they got into a car, with Jason driving, Max took off the bandage he'd put over the incision and applied some of the salve. Immediately, the wound felt warm and tingly, as if it was already mending.

Leaning into the crook of his arm, she watched the scene speeding by. It was so unbelievably green, so alive.

About twenty minutes later, they reached what Jason called the Randolph Research Facility.

"We thought you'd be comfortable here," he said as they drove through a locked gate that opened for them via a remote.

"Thank you," she answered, wondering if they had other reasons for keeping her in this isolated place. Maybe after the way she'd acted on the plane, they thought she was dangerous. And truthfully, she didn't believe that evaluation was far wrong.

A long, low building appeared around a bend in the road. It didn't look impressive from the outside. But inside it was warm and comfortable, with rugs on the floors and paintings on the walls.

More people, including a man named Zeke Chambers, who looked like he might be a scholar, were waiting to meet her in a large room with tables and chairs and couches. There was also an enormous television and something she knew was a pool table.

She turned to find Max and saw that he had in his hand the little bag with the thing that had been under her skin. He handed it to Thorn.

"If you don't mind, I'd like to run some tests on it," Thorn said politely.

"Please," she answered, because it might be the key to who she was.

Kathryn Kelley took her arm. "So, do you feel up to talking to us now?" she asked.

What Annie wanted to do was run and hide, but that wasn't an option, so she murmured her agreement.

"Then let's get comfortable." Kathryn led her to a couch.

Thorn took the plastic bag off somewhere, but everybody else settled onto the couches, where they could look at one another and also out the window at a garden with big stone statues and tall grasses. Max sat next to Annie, his arm around her.

A gray ball of fur on one of the couches lifted its head and looked at her with its strange yellow eyes.

"A cat," she breathed. "Can I touch it?"

"Harriet is very selective about who pets her," Max answered. Reaching out a hand, he let the animal sniff him. When it licked him with a pink tongue, he grinned, then scratched the animal's head.

She imitated Max's greeting ritual. When the animal didn't bite her, she stroked the fur on its broad back. "So soft," she murmured.

She leaned back, smoothing the cat's fur, liking the feel of the animal. She was almost relaxed when Max's next words had her nerves jumping again.

"As we discussed over the phone, Annie—I gave her that name, by the way—is trying to figure out who she is and where she came from, and I don't think it's Kansas."

Everybody laughed. Except the subject of the comment, who only shrugged helplessly.

"You don't get the reference?" Zeke asked.

She shook her head, feeling miserable. But she wasn't going to pretend.

"It's from *The Wizard of Oz,*" he said.

As he named the children's book, a line of description leaped into her head. "Dorothy and her little dog Toto get swept up in a tornado and end up in the land of Oz."

"You memorized that?"

"I must have. But I don't remember."

"Dorothy was from Kansas," Zeke explained. "So 'We're not in Kansas' has become a kind of standard comment when you're lost in a weird place."

"I see," she answered.

Max stroked her arm as he looked around the room. Maybe he was trying to make her feel better when he said, "I think that if anyone can help Annie, this group of misfits can do it."

"Thanks," Cassie muttered.

"Cassie excepted," Max said easily. "She's perfectly normal. A travel agent who uses her job as a cover for spying. But let's get back on track. I haven't told you how Annie and I met. I was fishing near the entrance to Hermosa Harbor, and she fell into the water.

"At the time I assumed she fell off the bridge that goes over the channel. Actually, I thought some drug dealer had pushed her off. But now I figure I was wrong. Just before she appeared, the air felt strange. It smelled like ozone. And there was a clap of thunder followed by lightning."

He stopped and looked around the room. All eyes were focused on him, and he cleared his throat. "If you want to know what I think now, I believe she fell out of the sky somehow. When we were on the plane coming here, she had an anxiety attack. Which leads me to conclude she might have been dropped out of some kind of vehicle without a parachute.''

Annie felt her stomach twist into painful knots. She was ready for everybody to look at her as if she was a freak. But nobody's expression changed.

Zeke turned to her and said, ''Well, there are a number of theories we could explore. I'm a linguist, and one thing I can deduce from your accent is that you're not from twenty-first-century America. And Max told me that you call binoculars knockers. That's an interesting variant of the word.''

''Max thought I acted like someone who came from a past century,'' Annie said.

''Unlikely. But the word *knockers* suggests that you come from a repressive society. One where sexuality gets channeled into crude references.''

''Yes,'' she agreed, because that had a ring of truth.

Jason came forward with a question for Max. ''You saw no plane or a helicopter?''

''Right,'' Max replied.

''So let's think about what other reasons there might be for someone falling out of the sky,'' Jason said.

Annie tipped her head to the side. ''I'm Chicken Little.'' Everyone laughed, and she liked that.

Zeke spoke up. ''Let's try some other theories. For example, you could be from another time continuum.''

''A what?'' Annie asked.

''A parallel universe. A universe that runs alongside this one, but some of our events turned out differently. Like the U.S. didn't invade Iraq. Or the Germans won World War II.''

''The U.S. did invade Iraq. And the Germans didn't win World War II,'' Annie said quickly. ''At least, those are facts I know,'' she said, marveling that these people were discussing the subject so calmly.

''You could have dropped from a spaceship,'' a voice said from behind Annie.

She whirled around to find Thorn Devereaux standing in the doorway.

Annie's heart started to pound in her chest. ''How can you think something so preposterous?'' she asked.

''Well, in the first place, I always keep an open mind when I deal with scientific facts. I've examined that little piece of plastic that came out of your body. It's a sophisticated computer. I think Max was correct in inferring that it was, to a certain extent, controlling your behavior. And whatever else it is, it's based on technology that's not available in the U.S. today.''

''It couldn't have been made in a secret government lab?'' Max asked sharply.

''I doubt it.''

''What about the Russians?'' Jed Prentiss asked.

''Forget the Russians,'' Thorn answered. ''They don't have the resources.''

''So you really believe in space aliens?'' Annie asked Thorn.

He laughed. ''Well, since I *am* a space alien, I guess so.''

Her jaw dropped open. ''That's a joke, right?''

He shook his head. ''It's a long story. But I came here from another planet.'' He walked to his wife and stood behind her. When he rested his palm on her shoulder, she reached up and covered his hand with hers. ''Cassie found me and saved my life. If it weren't for her, I would be dead.''

Annie watched the couple touching, exchanging a warm look, and she felt a pang of envy. Like the men and women she'd seen at the nightclub, they were open in their affection. The public display at Nicki's Paradise had embarrassed her, and she still had trouble watching lovers touch each other. But what she was seeing was different from the sexual atmosphere at the nightclub. Thorn and Cassie loved each other. It was hard for her to use that word, even in her mind. But she could see it in their eyes, in their touch. And she wanted that closeness with Max, even if it was forbidden.

Forbidden.

She swallowed, feeling her throat burn.

Forbidden by whom?

"What is it?" Kathryn Kelley asked, and Annie realized that the other woman had been watching her observe Thorn and Cassie.

"I was just…" She let her voice trail off because she couldn't reveal anything so personal.

"Let's get back to the problem of your identity," Kathryn said briskly, and Annie was grateful that the woman wasn't going to press her.

"Do you have a theory—besides space aliens?" Zeke asked Thorn.

"The most likely explanation is that she's from the future," the researcher said.

"Oh," Annie breathed, feeling her heart lurch.

"Think about it," Thorn continued. He turned to Max, "Annie told you she has a mission—something important she has to do."

"When the governor of Florida goes to Sea Kingdom," she said in a voice she could barely control.

"So maybe she was sent back by some technology we don't have yet so she could change the past. And to make sure she carried out her mission, they put a computer inside her. A computer with a self-destruct mechanism.''

''As in destroy itself?'' Max asked sharply.

''Yes. And destroy her,'' Thorn said. ''At the end of the assignment.''

Annie felt a wave of cold sweep over her.

Max's expression had turned angry. ''They don't sound like very nice folks,'' he muttered.

''Or they're desperate,'' Thorn countered. ''They need something done and they don't want to leave any evidence.''

''So what do they want from her?'' Jed cut in.

''I'd like to know,'' Max growled.

They talked for half an hour longer but could come to no conclusions.

Finally, Max turned to Annie. ''You look terrible,'' he said.

''Thank you.''

''You had anesthetic this morning. You need to rest.''

''All right,'' she agreed, glad he hadn't mentioned the scene on the plane.

Kathryn gestured toward the hall. ''Let me show you where you're going to be staying.''

Annie stood. So did Max. When she swayed slightly, he caught her arm and held her against his side.

She felt strange because everyone was looking at them. Yet at the same time, she liked having these people know that Max cared about her.

Kathryn led them toward a wing of the building that she explained housed the sleeping quarters.

''We understood that you didn't come with any luggage. So in the room you'll find clothing and anything else we thought you'd need.''

"Thanks," Max told her, and the tone of his voice made Annie suspect that he'd expected no less.

Kathryn stopped by a room and opened the door. Annie and Max followed her inside. Beyond a sliding glass door was interesting greenery. Not as colorful as the gardens she'd seen in Florida, but still pleasing to the eye.

"I've put you in adjoining quarters," Kathryn was saying. "This is Annie's room." She looked at Max. "You're through that connecting door. I hope that's all right."

"Fine," Max said.

Kathryn glanced at him. "Could you leave us alone for a while?"

Annie felt a jolt of panic. Yet when Max looked at her, she gave a small nod.

He left them standing in the middle of the room, with Annie clasping her hands nervously.

CHARLES ADJUSTED the sun hat on his brown hair and looked out at the crowd of men, women and children enjoying the Florida afternoon. He had nothing against them in particular. They hadn't chosen to be born into this godforsaken society. But they had come here to play, and they would suffer the consequences of being at the wrong place at the wrong time.

Well, not these exact same people. Unless they came back to Sea Kingdom for a few more days of fun in the sun.

He ambled down a path, then stopped to buy a cup of ice-cold lemonade from a vendor. Fresh-squeezed. The best kind.

He paid for the drink, then returned to the path. As he sipped his drink, he looked around the park.

He was scouting locations now. He was pretty sure where he was going to do it. But he had time to pick his spot. Not in the hall where the governor was speaking. Out here in the open air where more people would die.

He was dressed like a tourist today. Nobody knew him. He wasn't even on the FBI radar. He should be on the Ten Most Wanted list. But they had overlooked him.

Until now. He was going to be famous after this week. When it was already too late. He would go down in the history books. He liked that. He would die, but he would have a special immortality as one of the best-known men of the twenty-first century. Of all time, really.

He looked into his heart and saw only a cold steadiness. He was as ready as he was ever going to be. He'd bribed his way into an excellent disguise. Tonight he was scheduled to meet the man who was selling him what he needed. Then all he had to do was relax and wait for the governor's scheduled visit. Of course, he could do it before that, if he wanted. But he would probably wait. Because he liked the elegance of the plan the way he'd worked it out.

"WHY DON'T YOU sit down?" Kathryn said.

That was all the invitation Annie needed to drop into one of the easy chairs by the window.

Kathryn moved to the side of the room, where she picked up a small box from the dresser. "How about a nice, nourishing piece of chocolate?"

Annie wasn't sure how to respond. The definition of chocolate flitted through her mind, just as so many other references had come to her, but it wasn't anything she remembered personally.

Kathryn opened the box and held it out. Inside were little brown-paper containers each one with an individual square inside, some light brown and some darker. They didn't look very appealing, but Annie picked up one of the darker ones and took a bite. It was like nothing she had ever tasted. Even better than the butterscotch sundae that Max had fixed.

Kathryn was watching her closely. "Have another."

"I don't want to make a pork of myself."

"A pig," Kathryn corrected. "But it takes one to know one," she added quickly as she took a chocolate for herself.

Annie watched her enjoying the treat. "Do you feel guilty about eating that?" she asked.

"Well, I worry that it'll make me gain weight. But I don't feel like I'm taking anything away from starving orphans," she said as she took the other chair by the window.

"Everything here—the food, the pictures on the walls, the people—is a…good surprise to me."

"If I had to guess, I'd say you come from a spartan environment."

"What does that mean?"

"A place where the food isn't plentiful or particularly good-tasting. A place that doesn't look very attractive. An uncomfortable place where personal relationships are discouraged."

Annie's head shot up. "I guess I know how you can come to some of those conclusions. But how do you know anything about relationships?"

"I saw you watching Thorn and Cassie."

Annie felt embarrassment heat her face.

"And I saw how you are with Max. You want to be close to him. But you don't feel quite right about it."

"I must be pretty transparent."

"Not to everyone. But I'm a psychologist. Seeing what's below the surface of people is part of my job."

Annie lowered her gaze.

"Does that bother you?" Kathryn asked.

"Well, I feel like I can't hide much from you." She sighed. "So you may as well tell me—how do I get Max to make love with me?"

"Let him know that's what you want to do."

Again she felt heat creep into her cheeks. "I have. He says that he'd be taking advantage of me. Do you think that means he doesn't want to be intimate with me?"

"Do you?"

"He...he..." She stopped and clamped her hands around the chair arms.

"You don't have to go into any details," Kathryn said softly. "Just give him a chance to show you what he's feeling. He had a rough time after his wife died. He's cautious about relationships. But from what I can see, he cares about you. It would have been a lot easier to leave you in Florida than to take that computer thing out of you and bring you here."

Annie nodded, hanging on the woman's words.

"You should get some rest," Kathryn said. "We have dinner at eight here. I'll see you then, if you don't need anything else now."

"No. I'm fine." Annie hesitated, then blurted, "In the nightclub where we were waiting to find out about the drug shipment, women were wearing color on their faces. Is there some here that I can use? Can you show me how to put it on?"

"Of course."

They both went into the bathroom where Kathryn

demonstrated the use of eye makeup, blusher and lip-
stick. "You could use foundation, too. But I don't think
you need it."

Annie peered at herself in the mirror, "This looks
pretty," she murmured.

"Very pretty."

"Do you think Max will like it?"

"Yes."

"Thank you very much."

Kathryn smiled. "It was fun."

When Kathryn had left, Annie briefly explored the
bedroom. The closet was full of garments that she suspected would look good on her.

After pulling off her clothing in the bathroom, she
held up her arm and inspected the place where Max had
cut the computer from under her skin. To her amaze-
ment, the incision was almost impossible to see. Apparently he had been right about the healing properties
of Thorn's salve.

Once she'd showered and washed her hair, instead of
pulling on a T-shirt, she reached for a silky beige nightgown. It had lace at the bodice, a fitted waist and a skirt
that fell gracefully around her legs.

The fabric felt wonderful against her skin. So did the
clean sheets on the double bed in her room.

Snuggling under the covers, she let go of all the worries that had been plaguing her. She was safe here.
Warm and comfortable. She could sleep peacefully.

Her self-protective instincts came surging back when
the mattress shifted. Her hand shot up, but Max caught
it.

"Is that how you react when someone tries to wake
you?" he asked, a teasing note in his voice.

"I'm sorry. I guess my training kicks in even without that thing under my arm."

"How does the incision feel?"

"Fine. I looked at it before I took a shower. You'd hardly know." She pushed herself up, then saw that Max's gaze had dropped to the front of her gown, and the warmth in his eyes made her breasts tighten. Somehow she kept from folding her arms across her chest.

He looked as if he was going to reach for her. Instead, he took a step back.

"You need to get ready for dinner."

To her embarrassment, the mention of food made her stomach growl, and she realized she hadn't eaten much all day. "What do the women wear at dinner here?" she asked.

"The same clothes they were wearing at that meeting we had. I'll see you down the hall in the lounge."

She nodded, waiting until he'd closed the door before she got out of bed.

Then she dressed quickly in a green shirt and dark pants. In the bathroom she brushed on a little of the makeup Kathryn had shown her how to use.

Feeling nervous, she made her way slowly down the hall. Max was talking to Jed, but he apparently had one eye on the hallway. The warm look he gave her told her that he liked the effect of the makeup.

"Come try Zeke's salmon spread," he said. "Zeke is a gourmet cook. He loves an excuse to show off his skills." Max scooped something creamy onto a cracker and handed it to her.

Like everything else she'd tasted since coming here, it was wonderful. And she made sure she told that to Zeke.

After dinner, some of the men settled down in front

of the television to watch a basketball game. Others went back to their rooms.

"Do you want to see the gardens?" Max asked.

When she nodded, he left her for a moment and came back with a light knit covering, which he draped around her shoulders. Then he led her through a set of double doors. It had gotten dark, but floodlights illuminated the gardens. They wandered slowly down a path that curved gently through the greenery, then to a wooden bridge where a stream rushed over and around huge boulders. The sky was navy-blue, with a few faint streaks of pink and orange.

Annie dragged in a draft of pure, fresh air. "It even smells good here."

"You're smelling the pine trees." Max stroked her cheek. "You could stay here," he said. "I mean, you don't have to go back to Florida. With your training, Randolph Security would give you a job." He laughed. "Most of the agents—me included—have come here from stressful careers."

"Your wife was killed on a mission," she said softly.

"Yes, she was."

"Do you miss her?"

"I did. I was kind of self-destructive after she died. I've got my head screwed on right again." Without skipping a beat, he switched the subject to her. "We can send agents to Florida who can work with the state police. You don't have to take the responsibility. Other people can guard the governor."

She was truly tempted, thinking that it would be wonderful to turn the job over to someone else. But she couldn't.

"I'd like to do it," she murmured.

"You don't sound convinced."

"Somebody gave me the responsibility. If Thorn is right, they sent me back here because they thought it was vitally important."

"If Thorn is right, they're not very nice. And they certainly screwed up. You arrived here with no idea of what you were supposed to do. You still don't know."

She sighed. "All of that is correct. But I'm not sure I can just walk away from the job they gave me."

"Even if they intended for you to die afterward?"

The words and the sharp tone of his voice made her cringe.

"I'm sorry," he said instantly. "I shouldn't have said that."

"But it's true." She looked down, watching a leaf caught in the current. The stream was carrying it along, over rocks and down a small waterfall, and it had no choice where it was going. "It's something I need to consider. But my head is still spinning from what I've already learned."

"I understand." He reached for her hand, holding tight. For long moments, they stood looking at the water. It was so beautiful here. So safe. And this man beside her wanted her to enjoy it all with him.

It would be easy to agree. Yet doubt gnawed her insides. When she dropped her guard, terrible images gathered in her head. Images of hundreds of dead people. Thousands. And if she stayed here with Max, she would be responsible for their deaths.

Footsteps coming down the path made them both look up to see Thorn walking rapidly toward them.

"I was looking for you," he called.

"You found us," Max said, sounding as though he wasn't too pleased by the interruption.

"I've been running some computer simulations," Thorn said, addressing Annie. "There may be a way to get your memory back. But there could be some risk to you."

Chapter Fifteen

"Absolutely not!" Max said, fighting the fear that grabbed him by the throat.

He felt Annie's hand clamp on his, and he clung to her because he suddenly felt unsteady on his feet.

"Let me at least hear what he has to say," she whispered.

He wanted to shout that Thorn had just started and finished his presentation. But he figured she wouldn't react well to his coming down on the researcher like a gorilla. Somehow he managed to keep his voice low and steady as he said, "You can hear him out, but I'm not going to let you do anything risky."

Thorn remained impassive. "Why don't we go back to my lab?"

They didn't speak again as they retraced their steps along the path, then into the building through a side door. Thorn ushered them through a small, cluttered office into a spotless lab with computers and medical equipment. What made Max's stomach clench was a padded table near one wall. Wires were attached from it to a computer.

"What the hell is that?" he asked, pointing toward the table, wondering if he really wanted to hear the answer. But maybe it would frighten Annie enough to get her out of here.

Thorn turned to face him. "You've heard of electro-shock treatments?"

"Yeah, they're given to patients with severe depression."

"Right."

"Do you know those treatments often destroy the patient's memory?"

Max nodded.

"Well, I've been working with some doctors at the Haversham Clinic in Baltimore. We're trying to come up with a procedure that will reverse that memory loss."

Max snorted. He couldn't keep the sarcasm out of his voice as he said, "Have you had any success?"

"We haven't tested it on a patient yet."

"Oh, yeah, right. But I get the feeling you want to use Annie as a guinea pig."

She put a hand on his arm. "Let him explain what he's doing," she said gently.

Max gave her a dark look, then pressed his lips together because he knew he wasn't doing himself any good.

Thorn began lecturing on the nature of memory and electrical activity within the brain.

When he finished, Max managed not to issue a curse before saying, "I don't like it."

"It's not up to you," the researcher said mildly. He looked at Annie. "What do *you* think?"

Max couldn't breathe as he waited for her answer.

"It has a chance of restoring my memory?"

"But it's risky!" Max almost shouted.

"How risky? What could happen?" she asked.

At least Thorn didn't lie about it. "It could destroy your present memories. It could do something we haven't anticipated. There's always a risk when you're dealing with the human brain."

Max slung an arm around Annie and wedged her against his side.

"I'll have to think about it," she said.

"I understand," Thorn answered. "I just wanted to introduce the idea to you. We can talk more about it later. And probably you'll have some questions for me."

"Let's get out of here," Max said, tugging her along with him as he strode out of the lab. His chest was so tight he could barely breathe.

"Slow down," Annie begged, and he felt a stab of guilt. This morning he had drugged her and dug a computer-like device out of her flesh. Now he was racing her along the corridors as though the devil were in pursuit. Slowing his pace, he tried to decide which of their two bedrooms would be best. Finally, he led her into his room and closed the door behind them.

Because he wanted maximum privacy, he walked toward the double patio doors and pulled the curtains, completely obliterating the moonlight.

He turned to find Annie watching him. He'd thought that taking out that damn implant had made her safe— until Thorn had given him the scare of his life. If he knew anything, he knew that he couldn't risk losing this woman. The more he knew about her, the more important she became to him.

She had to stay in his life. And he had to make her understand what he was feeling.

"Annie," he said, unable to stop himself from closing the space between them and pulling her into his arms.

It was a relief that she molded her body to his, cleaved to him.

He didn't know what to say. He wasn't sure that talking would do him any good, anyway. So he lowered his head and ravaged her mouth, feeling the edge of desperation in the kiss, feeling as if he were drowning, with no one to save him except the woman in his arms.

"Hold on to me, honey," he murmured, his words warm against her lips.

She did as he asked, tightening her arms around his waist.

His hands ran possessively up and down her back as he deepened the kiss, giving her everything he could, yet taking at the same time. Because he was so damn needy.

He had told himself he wouldn't make love with her until she knew him better. Until she knew this world better.

But now fear had driven him past any kind of normal need. He had wanted her since the night when she'd so sweetly let him give her pleasure. Wanted her with an urgency that frightened him. Now he felt his heart slamming against the walls of his chest as he gathered her in.

The taste of her was intoxicating. The feel of her mouth on his, the pressure of her breasts against his chest were exquisite.

The way her hips rubbed his erection drove every thought out of his mind—save two. He must have her. And he must keep her safe.

In some deeply, buried part of his mind, he knew he was pushing her too fast. But it was beyond his power to turn her loose. Not when she was making small, enticing sounds in her throat, begging him to take her where they both wanted to go. He knew he would go out of his mind if he didn't show her what he felt for her tonight. Tonight and every other night for the rest of his life.

He felt her trembling in his arms, which brought back a small measure of sanity.

Lifting his head, he said, "What the hell am I doing?"

"You're going to do what I asked for last night," she said in a voice as quivery as her body.

"Yeah, but not like this."

A mixture of relief and disappointment washed over her face. "Then how?" she asked in a barely audible voice.

"With a little more finesse." He loosened his grip on her, then dragged in a breath. "I guess I'd better ask. Is having sexual intercourse what you want to do?"

"Oh, yes."

"Then maybe you'll do something for me."

"Anything."

"Put on that nightgown you were wearing when I came into your room."

She blinked. "Why?"

"Because I liked seeing you in something sexy." Truthfully, he was thinking that her wearing it might slow him down a little. Or maybe while she was in the bathroom, she'd change her mind. He wanted to give her a chance to do that, not railroad her into bed.

The moment she exited through the connecting door, he took out a box of condoms from the bedside table. Next he dashed down the hall to the pantry, opened the refrigerator and got out a bottle of champagne, then filled an ice bucket and grabbed two flutes.

A couple of the guys made comments, but he ignored them, the same way he ignored the knowing gaze of Kathryn Kelley as he hurried back to the bedroom. He was wondering what *he* was going to wear. Lord, he was acting like a nervous groom on his wedding night, but he couldn't help it.

He rummaged in the dresser drawers and found a pair of nice silk pajama bottoms.

When Annie returned, he had just folded back the covers on the bed. His breath caught when he looked at her. She'd put on more makeup—as if she needed it.

"You're stunning," he said. And she looked more nervous than he did—which was some consolation.

She blushed. "I feel like a princess or something. I don't think I ever owned anything so sinfully rich feeling."

"It's not a sin. It's what you deserve." He stepped toward the dresser. "Like a nice glass of champagne. Why don't we have a drink?"

"What's champagne?"

"Something very good."

"Like chocolate?"

He smiled. "You be the judge."

With hands that felt suddenly stiff, he managed to get the cork out without its shooting across the room. Then he poured them each a flute.

"To us," he said, clinking his glass to hers, then taking a swallow.

She took a cautious sip. Her face changed as she absorbed the taste. "This is…sweet. And bubbly," she said. "Different from chocolate."

"Do you like it?"

She tried another sip. "Yes."

"I think you're not sure. But don't drink too much."

"Why not?"

"It will make you stop thinking clearly."

"Like White Bliss?"

"What's that?" he asked, keeping his voice steady, even though her casually spoken phrase had made his stomach lurch.

"Something people take to make them feel good," she said, then blinked.

"Something you remember?"

"Not something I used," she said quickly. "Something illegal. And expensive." She held up the glass. "Is this illegal?"

"No. And it's not out of my price range, either." He punctuated the remark with another sip. So did she.

"We'll save the rest for later," he said, lifting the glass out of her hand and setting it on the dresser, along with his.

When he looked back, he saw her glancing nervously around the room and knew when she spotted the box of condoms on the night table. Crossing the room, she picked up the box. "What is this?"

"That's what I'm going to use to keep you from getting pregnant."

She opened the box and took out a foil packet. She turned it in her hand and put it down again. "There was a box something like that in the bedroom where I was sleeping on your boat. I found it when I was searching the drawers."

"What were you looking for?"

"Clues to where I was. I guess, *when* I was."

He nodded solemnly, sorry he'd asked the question when her expression saddened. "What I'd like to do is make you stop worrying about anything that's happened and focus on being with me.''

''I'm worried about that, too.''

''Why?''

''I want to do this right.''

''There is no right. It's just what two people enjoy doing together.''

''You stopped a little while ago, because you thought you were doing it wrong.''

''I was going too fast for you,'' he said, pulling her into his arms, and kissing her cheek, nibbling her ear, her neck.

''That feels good,'' she breathed.

He tried not to think about how much he wanted her. Instead, he focused on her pleasure as he slipped one finger under a strap of her gown, caressed her shoulder, then dipped lower to the cleft between her breasts.

She made a small, purring sound, and he knew he was pleasing her.

He found the hardened tips of her breasts through the thin fabric of the bodice, teasing them with his fingers and then with his lips and teeth.

She arched into the caress, her hands gripping his shoulders.

Lifting her off her feet, he carried her to the bed.

''I think you'll be more comfortable without this,'' he murmured, sweeping the nightgown up and over her head, exposing her naked body.

Lying back against the turned-down covers, she looked up at him, slightly dazed. But she had the presence of mind to say, ''You, too. I want you naked, too.''

He compromised by taking off the pajama bottoms and leaving on his briefs, then followed her onto the bed and gathered her in his arms, sliding her body against his as he kissed her and stroked her back and the curve of her bottom.

"Are you really going to put that inside me?" she asked, her hand gliding between them and cupping around his erection.

"Oh, yeah."

"Don't you have to take off your underwear?"

He laughed. "Uh-huh. But not yet. The briefs will slow me down."

"I don't want you to slow down."

"Oh, it'll be more fun that way," he managed to say. "Trust me."

He kissed her gently, then with more heat as she accepted what he offered.

He reveled in the feel of her skin against his as he slipped a hair-roughened leg between her smooth ones, then began to caress her breasts again, starting at the outer margins, smiling as he watched her respond to his teasing touch.

He had never felt anything more perfect than what was happening between them in this bed. His own pleasure leaped to meet hers, yet it was so much less important than making this first time as perfect for her as he could. For he was surer than ever that she had never done this before.

He watched her drag in ragged gulps of air as she responded to his kisses and his caresses.

And when his fingers parted the folds of her most intimate flesh, he found her hot and slick and ready for him.

She had learned something from the last time they'd been together. Boldly, she slid her hand down his body and pushed his briefs away so she could close her fingers around him the way he had taught her.

His own breath went ragged, and he had to fight to keep from straining toward her.

"I want you to put this in me now," she whispered. "But you have to tell me how we do it."

"We can do what we did the last time," he forced himself to say.

"No. I want to make love with you the way men and women are supposed to fit together."

Oh, yes.

Quickly, he gave her instructions, then stripped off his underwear, reached for the packet she'd taken out and made himself ready, conscious of her gaze on him.

When he knelt between her knees, she looked up at him with such a mixture of longing and uncertainty that he almost lay back down beside her.

But she must have seen that in his face, because she reached out and gripped his shoulder. "Max, don't deny me this."

The emotion in her voice kept him where he was. He kissed her raised knee, then stroked her most sensitive flesh, bringing her close to orgasm again.

When he knew that he had her poised on the edge, he whispered, "The first time may hurt. But just for a moment."

"Okay," she breathed.

He moved into her slowly, pressing past the barrier, hearing her gasp.

Above her, he ordered himself to still. "Annie, are you all right?"

"Yes. Because I want you inside me like this." Her arms tightened around him, and she looked up into his face. "I want you to make me feel the way I did before," she whispered.

Hoping he had the skill to do that, he began to move inside her, watching her face, judging her reaction.

At first she looked tense, then she got into it, her hips rising and falling in opposition to his, her hands sliding possessively up and down his back.

He focused on her reactions, then wedged his hand between them, pressing against the place that would intensify her pleasure.

She cried out, and he felt her inner muscles contract around him.

He held back as long as he could, reveling in her soft cries. Then climax took over his body.

But his pleasure was never separate from hers. He felt as though a hot storm had carried them high above the treetops together, then gently set them down.

Annie clung to him, and he cradled her in his arms. He wanted to tell her how much he loved her. He wanted to ask her to marry him so he could keep her with him always. But he was afraid to overwhelm her.

So he simply pulled the covers around them and held her.

"I must come from a pretty awful place if they don't want people to feel that pleasure," she whispered.

He had no answer for her except, "You're here now. With me, where we can do this any time we want."

She gave him a dazzling smile, and that was enough for the moment.

SUNLIGHT KNIFED IN through the crack between the drapes when he awoke. He was alone in the bed. Craning his neck toward the bathroom, he saw that Annie wasn't in there.

In one fluid motion, he vaulted out of bed and

reached for his pants, all the time telling himself not to panic.

She had to be here somewhere. She couldn't have left the compound on her own. Or had she gotten somebody to fly her back to Florida? One other possibility made a sick feeling rise in his throat.

Barefoot, zipping his pants as he went, Max ran down the hall to Thorn's laboratory, cursing Annie, cursing himself for not making his intentions plain to her.

Another imprecation exploded from his lips when he saw Annie, dressed in a white hospital gown, strapped to the table. Thorn was at the nearby computer. Dr. Katie McQuade was leaning over her.

He would have burst into the room, but he knew he was too late, and he knew that if he interfered now, he could do more harm than good. So he watched helplessly through the door as Annie's body convulsed and then went still.

Chapter Sixteen

As if he knew the scene in the lab was being observed, Thorn turned toward the door. When he saw who was staring through the glass, he met Max's eyes.

As Max watched wordlessly, the researcher crossed the room and conferred with Katie. She glanced up, a look of regret on her face.

Somehow, that look was the last straw. If Katie didn't like what Annie was doing, that went double for Max.

Unable to stop himself, he flung open the door and surged into the room, his eyes flashing as he looked from Thorn and Katie to Annie, lying pale and unconscious on the table. Machinery beeped in the background, and he realized she was hooked up to monitoring equipment.

"How could you?" he demanded, pressing his palms hard against his thighs to keep from punching Thorn.

The researcher's face held a mixture of warring emotions. "Max, she came to me this morning. She told me that she had to find out what she'd been sent to our time period to do. She said she wanted so much to stay here with you, but she couldn't do it if her own happiness was going to consign thousands of people to death."

Max felt as if he'd been poleaxed. "She said all that?" he asked in a shaky voice.

Katie put a gentle hand on his arm. "Yes. Thorn called me in to be a witness."

Max bit out a string of raw words that he knew shouldn't be uttered in front of a lady. But he couldn't help himself.

"I'm sorry," Katie said. "Even with that computer removed from her body, she has a very strong sense of purpose. Of morality, actually. She thinks she was sent here to do something vitally important. Maybe even to save the world."

"Save the world!" Max cursed again. "How can one woman do that?"

"She says she has to try—that she can't just walk away from her responsibility."

"Even if the people who dragged her into their scheme planned to kill her?" Max said bitterly.

"I'm sorry," Katie repeated.

Max clenched and unclenched his hands. This was the nightmare he remembered, coming back to swallow him up again. He was living through hell once more. It was like when Stephanie had gone off on a mission and never returned.

Well, not exactly the same, he conceded. Stephanie had been obsessed with proving herself. Annie couldn't let go of her sense of duty.

Afraid of what he might discover, he walked toward her and looked down at her still body.

Katie said, "I gave her a thorough physical before we did anything. She's in very good health for someone who had an inadequate diet as a child."

"You can tell that?"

"Yes. But more importantly, her vital signs are stable now."

Max gave her a dark look. "And after you checked the state of her health, you let Thorn send an electric current into her brain."

"It's a little more complicated than that," the physician whispered. "But from a layman's point of view, I guess that's right."

"Is that responsible medicine? Using a human being as a guinea pig?"

"When the patient wants it," she said, but he could tell she wasn't entirely comfortable with the situation.

"When does she wake up?" Max demanded.

Katie glanced from Annie to the monitors. "We don't know."

He flapped his arm in frustration. "Oh, that's just great. Thank you so much." His voice dripped with sarcasm.

"We're going to move her to the recovery room," Thorn said.

"And you better believe I'm going to stay with her," Max growled.

They wheeled the table and the monitors into a smaller room and transferred Annie to a hospital bed. Max pulled a chair over to the bed and sat down, watching for any sign that she was going to wake up. But Annie didn't move. She didn't seem to know that he was there, even when he squeezed her hand.

Katie came in several times and checked her, always optimistic, professional. But as the hours wore on, Max could tell that the physician was worried. Later, when he came back from the men's room, he heard her and Thorn conferring in low voices. They looked at him, then glanced quickly away.

He closed his eyes, fighting the sick feeling that rose in his throat. Annie had to wake up. She had to! Because if she didn't, he was going to come apart. Just as he'd come apart after Stephanie. Then, his Light Street friends had brought him back. Today, he knew that wouldn't be possible. Not when they were the ones responsible for his loss.

It had been years since he'd prayed. Now, sitting beside Annie's bed, he began to say words that felt awkward on his lips. But he had to speak them.

"Please, God, please help her. She made a perilous journey. She's so brave and so sure that she's here on an important mission. I haven't asked you for much in my miserable life. But I'm asking now. Save her. Don't do it for me. Do it for her."

He wanted to howl in anguish. Instead, he reached for Annie's hand, his grip firm on her warm flesh, because there was nothing else he could do.

Katie came in quietly and checked the patient.

"Well?" he asked.

"She's stable."

"But there's no change?"

She shook her head. "I'm sorry. We don't have much experience with this."

He glared at Katie as she left the room.

Desperate, anguished, he spoke directly to Annie, hoping he could somehow break through to her. "Please, honey. Come back to me. You're so brave. So strong. And damn you, so foolish to put yourself in danger like this."

He sucked in a breath and let it trickle out of his lungs before he managed to say, "Annie, I love you. I should have told you that last night. But I didn't want to put any pressure on you. Well, I'm putting pressure on you now. Annie, wake up. For God's sake, don't do this to me.''

He felt so weary, as if all the strength had been sapped out of him. There was nothing left inside him and, still holding her hand, he leaned back in the chair and closed his eyes.

Sometime during the afternoon, Harriet the cat came in and curled up beside Annie as though lending support. Max didn't chase her away, although he was pretty sure no hospital would have allowed a cat to lie in bed with a patient.

Maybe having the animal close would help.

He was sitting with his eyes closed when he felt slender fingers press his hand.

He was instantly alert, his gaze shooting to Annie's face in time to see her eyelids flicker and finally open. Her confused expression turned crazed as though she was going to rip off the leads and monitors and bolt.

He felt the world fall out from under him. She was awake, but her mind was damaged.

''Annie! Oh, God, Annie.''

At the sound of his voice, her facial expression changed. ''Max?'' she whispered in a raspy voice.

''Yes. I'm here, honey. I'm here,'' he answered, thanking God that she knew who he was.

''Max, hold me. I feel him.'' She gasped. ''I don't want to feel him! Just please hold me.''

He did as she asked, standing and clasping her to him. She lay still for heartbeats. Then her arms crept up, circling his back.

''Oh, Max,'' she breathed. ''Oh, Max. It's awful.''

Leaning over her, he kissed her cheek, her brow. Then he gently brushed her lips with his. When he straightened, her hand clutched at him.

"Don't leave me," she whispered.

"Never."

She sobbed, and the sad look on her face tore at him.

"What?" he asked. "Tell me what's wrong."

"Carp," she answered. "I know what it means. I know why it's a curse word in my time."

"Why?"

"It's because of Charles Carpenter," she gasped. "I feel him." She stopped, took a breath. "He's going to release the virus when the governor goes to Sea Kingdom." Panic flared on her face. "How long have I been unconscious? How long do we have?"

Unbeknownst to them, Katie had come in. "You're disturbing her," she said to Max.

Annie turned to her. "No! He's not disturbing me. He has to help me. Charles Carpenter is going to do it. And I have to stop him. How much time do I have?" she asked again, terrible urgency in her voice.

"If you mean, when is the governor going to Sea Kingdom, you've got two days."

She moaned again. "I have to—"

"You have to rest, because if you're in this kind of shape, you won't be able to do anything."

Annie closed her eyes, then opened them and looked pleadingly at Katie. "Can't you give me something to make me okay?"

"Not now. You have to rest," the physician said, echoing Max.

Annie looked as if she wanted to leap off the bed.

Max put a hand on her shoulder. "Do I have to tie you down?"

She sighed. But she must have seen the determination in his eyes because she said, "No."

He fought to tamp down his own fears. When she

licked her dry lips, he asked, "do you want some water?"

"Yes."

He picked up a glass and held a straw to her lips. Just sucking in a little water seemed to tire her.

"We'll talk about Sea Kingdom later," he murmured.

She looked pleadingly at him. "Not later. You don't understand. I remember it all now. And it's…it's a miracle I can tell you about it. Remember before that I got a headache when you tried to break through my memory?"

He nodded. "When I hypnotized you."

"Yes. My head hurt so much then." She looked at Katie. "I guess whatever Thorn did changed something in my brain. I mean, I have my memory back. And…and I can tell you what I remember. You must have broken the block my Handlers put in me. I can talk about it now."

"Your Handlers?" Max asked carefully. "What the hell do you mean?"

She looked at him, her gaze piercing. "The people who trained me. They were called Handlers. They were the ones who did…something to me so I can open locks. Like on the handcuffs and at the storage shed. They sent me here. And what I have to tell you is so bad you probably won't believe me. Not when your world is so different. But I come from—" she stopped and seemed to gather her resolve "—well, about two hundred years in the future. You can't imagine what it's like. Pollution. Not enough food. The squads hunt down illegal children and kill them, because only a few people are allowed to have babies at all. People whose genes are undamaged. That's…that's why we are taught to think sex is nasty.''

''Then what about dime girls?'' he asked.

Her face darkened. ''There are men who have the credits to pay… We don't talk about those things. There are a lot of things we don't talk about. Like what happens to illegal children. But I know, because…of Suli.''

She stopped for a moment, apparently gathering her strength. ''Momma hid us. But they found us. They took us to the holding pens. I was okay. But not Suli.''

''Your sister?''

''Yes. I told you. Before they took Momma away, she begged me to watch out for Suli. But I couldn't. They killed her.''

The guilt in her voice made him reach for her and fold her close. ''You couldn't do anything. You were just a kid, weren't you?''

''Yes,'' she whispered. ''But it doesn't make me feel good about it.''

He was trying to grapple with everything she had said, trying to imagine the horror she'd lived through. Trying to imagine how it had affected her.

Then she began talking again. ''Max, it all started when Governor Bradley went to Sea Kingdom. That's in the history files. My history. That's when Charles Carpenter released a genetically engineered virus. People from all over the country were there. People from around the world. They took it home with them, and there were outbreaks everywhere. Most people who got it died. The world population was decimated. And the world fell apart. Your world. There were riots. Panic. The police couldn't handle it. Everything started going to hell. We had to put on a P-suit just to go out of the caves. A suit like I was wearing when I arrived here.''

"You pulled the helmet off," he said, remembering when he'd first seen her.

"Yes. I felt like I was suffocating."

He stared down at her. He remembered the suit, but that didn't make her story true.

His expression must have told her he was having trouble believing. Urgently, she went on, "You know I'm afraid of loud noises. You remember how I went into a panic when that smoke alarm went off. Well, that's like the alarm when the raiders come. The raiders who live outside the complex and are all sick and half-crazy from the air they breathe. They come in to kill as many of us as they can and steal what they can. I used to be terrified of the alarm when I was a kid. In the boat, when I couldn't remember my past, I guess I got that mixed up with all the people who died from the virus."

She looked down at the cat and stroked its soft gray fur, then looked back at Max. "There is nothing soft or nice in my world. No cats. If there were, someone would eat it, not pet it."

Max clung to her free hand, still struggling to take in her story.

"You don't believe me," she said in a weary voice. "If you won't help me, I'll have to go down there and try to stop him myself."

"I believe you," Thorn said from the doorway.

All heads turned toward him.

"Why?" she asked in a thin voice.

"Because you have antibodies in your blood that are protecting you against a disease that doesn't yet exist." He looked at Max. "A disease that would have killed her long ago if she didn't have the protection."

Max felt his breath catch. "You're sure?"

"Oh, yes."

"Then what the hell are we going to do?"

"Help her stop Charles Carpenter," Thorn said.

"Thank you," Annie breathed, then looked down at her hospital gown. "I need to get dressed. We need to have another meeting, so I can tell everybody what I know." She looked from Max to Thorn and back again. "You may decide that you don't want to help me, that it's too dangerous."

"We'll help you," Max said. He was pretty sure the rest of the people here would go along with him, too. If they wouldn't, he'd do it himself. Because he knew Annie was going down to that damn theme park unless the sky fell first, and he wasn't going to let her do it alone.

BERT TRAINER looked at the remains of his lunch spread on the motel-room table. Southern fried chicken. One of his favorites. But today he hadn't been able to do justice to the "secret spice" combination. What he *had* eaten wasn't sitting well in his stomach.

In the background, the TV was playing a promo loop of area attractions. Even with the sound turned down, it was annoying. But he kept it on as he crossed to the dressing table, shook an antacid out of the bottle and popped it into his mouth.

As he chewed it, he stuffed the leftover lunch into a paper bag. He'd been taking stomach medications for years. Now they were doing little to calm the roiling in his gut. He'd felt sick ever since the DEA had scooped up Nicki Armstrong and Hap Henderson. But he'd escaped. He'd been lucky.

"Lucky Bert," he muttered aloud.

He'd led a charmed life for the past thirty years, since

he'd arrived in Florida. He had a job he loved, a nice source of extra money, a lot of it socked away in a Swiss bank account. A comfortable little house. Women who gave him free sex. All the amenities he'd come to crave.

Somehow he'd convinced himself that it could go on forever. Or at least until he died a natural death. But Annie Oakland's arrival had shaken him out of his daydream. He'd found a one-piece suit under the bunk in the small cabin of *The Wrong Stuff*. He wanted to ask her about that and a lot of other things.

He wanted to interrogate the living hell out of her. Make her come clean about why she was here in Florida. But she and Max Dakota had cleared out of Hermosa Harbor too fast, although they'd left some nice, convenient notes. Which raised an interesting question. Were the notes for real? Or had they been planted to raise his blood pressure?

He growled a curse. They didn't know who he was. They couldn't know.

But who in the name of the saints was Max Dakota, anyway? Bert had thought the guy was in town to snoop into the drug business—maybe as an investor. It had been hard to pin him down. Now it looked as if the whole performance could have been a smoke screen.

Maybe he'd been in Florida all along waiting for Annie. But why? How did he know about her?

Bert closed his eyes, then blinked them open as the Sea Kingdom part of the promo came on. Unwillingly, he walked across the room and turned up the sound. Sitting on the edge of the bed, he studied the park—the crowds, the buildings, the huge outdoor water tanks.

But watching it on TV didn't substitute for the real thing. As soon as his stomach felt better, he was going over there to look around.

KATIE CLEARED the room so Annie could get dressed while Max hurried off to tell everyone about the developments.

Twenty minutes later, when Annie entered the lounge dressed in sweatpants and a T-shirt, and still not quite sure of her footing, the group applauded her.

She stopped, looking startled, then flustered.

Max got up and steadied her, then led her to one of the couches.

"Why are they clapping?" she asked him in a low voice.

"Because they know what you've been through. Because they know how brave you are."

"I'm not brave. I'm scared."

"That's okay," he said. "Being scared is okay." He longed to whisk her off where they could talk privately about the two of them. But he'd come to understand any plans he had for them must be put on hold, because the future was going to be pretty grim if Charles Carpenter succeeded in releasing the virus.

Annie looked pale as she sat on the sofa. Max handed her a decaf latte laced with butterscotch syrup.

He watched her take a sip, relished the look of pleasure on her face.

"Feeding you is so gratifying," he murmured.

"This has some of that butterscotch?" she asked.

"Yeah."

She sighed and took another sip. "You don't know how lucky you are to be able to eat this way."

He nodded, then looked up to see the others taking

it in. And he knew that they were getting the point he'd made.

She drank several more sips, licked her lips, then set down the mug. "I'm not used to…to lecturing."

"Take your time," Jed Prentiss said.

She gave him a grateful look, then smiled as Harriet dashed toward her, jumped up on the couch and settled down beside her.

"She likes me!"

"She has good taste," Max said.

Annie stroked the cat's gray fur. "She made that noise before. What is it?"

"She's purring. That's how she says she's happy."

Annie bent to the cat for a few more moments, then looked up at the people turned expectantly toward her.

He saw her swallow. But she didn't flinch as she began to speak—starting with a very good analogy.

"I want to tell you about a virus," she said, "something a lot worse than that anthrax attack you all know about."

That got everybody's attention. She went on to tell them what she'd already told Max and Katie, adding what Thorn had said about the antibodies.

Max watched her and watched the other people in the room, judging their reactions. They seemed to be staying with her.

"I've never heard of Charles Carpenter," Jason Zacharias said when she finally wound down. "What's his motivation?"

"He belongs to a group that wants to bring down the U.S. government. We think he picked the day the governor visited the park to make a point."

"How did he get the virus?"

"From a laboratory operating in what you call the Middle East."

"What do you call it?" Max asked.

"The poison zone."

That got their attention.

"But if Carpenter's spreading the virus, won't it kill him, too?" Katie asked.

Annie swallowed hard. "It's a suicide mission. Like mine—only I didn't know it."

Max gripped her hand, and she clung to him in the sudden silence.

Jed cleared his throat. "Why can't we just tell the police? Can't they scoop him up?"

"They won't know who he is. He'll release the virus before they can stop him."

"How will *you* know Carpenter?"

She spread her hands. "My Handlers tied me to him. With something they called a touchstone."

Max could see that she'd just lost her audience. "You have to explain that," he said gently.

"They had DNA material from him. In one of their first experiments, they sent a probe back to collect it. The capsule was waiting for them, in my time. They grafted some of his cells onto me, to sensitize me. I can't explain what that means, exactly. But when I get close to him, I'll know who he is. I guess it wasn't supposed to activate until near the day of the virus attack." She clenched and unclenched her hands. "I can feel him now. Just a little. I'm too far away to know where he is." She looked at Max. "That's what I meant when I woke up."

He nodded, wondering how the others were reacting to her explanation.

She was obviously wondering the same thing. "I

know it's a lot to believe," she murmured. "You have to take it on faith, because I can't prove it to you."

"Given future technology, it's possible," Jed said slowly.

"And if she's right, we have to try to stop him," Jason added.

Max wanted to get up and hug the two men, but he stayed beside Annie.

"Ten years ago," Annie continued, "our scientists came up with the plan to send somebody back to stop Carpenter. They've been trying to make it work for five years. I know they sent people before me," she said. "But nothing has changed. They think maybe they arrived at the wrong time. Too early. Or too late. Or someone was sent to prevent the mission from succeeding."

"Who would do that? Who would know?"

She shrugged. "I can't tell you. But they were afraid I'd be stopped. They warned me I had to operate in secret."

"Perhaps the agents they sent didn't remember their mission," Thorn speculated. "Perhaps the process of sending someone back in time erases memory."

"Is it just women?" Max asked.

"No. There were five men before me."

"Why'd they choose you?" Jason asked.

She dipped her head, then gave him a direct look. "I was trained as a guard in one of the residential complexes. I was good at my job. But I got into trouble. There was a man who…kept trying to do things with me that were…forbidden. I didn't like him, but I couldn't get away from him." She stopped, looked down at her hands. "It's hard for me to talk about… private things. We're…I guess you'd call us puritanical.'' She looked at Max, and he silently told her that anything she said now was okay.

"We were seen together and arrested,'' she said softly, then spoke more strongly. "I had a choice. I could go to one of the colonies where they're trying to expand our territory or I could accept this mission. The colonies are not a good place to live. So I said I would come here. When they started training me, I wanted to back out, but I couldn't. There was a lot of preparation. I learned so much about your world. I couldn't believe it all.''

"Like what?'' Max asked.

"They told me that children play games like hide-and-seek. And football. They told me mothers and fathers pick each other. That they live together. Then you told me some of those things, Max. I wanted to hear as much about it as I could.''

Max squeezed her hand. He saw that her eyes were watering. He couldn't imagine what she'd been through in her life. In her training. In coming here.

"You need to rest now,'' he said. "We'll talk about the best way to get you into Sea Kingdom and how to protect you when you're there. I promise we'll get Carpenter.''

She nodded, and he was pretty sure she believed him.

"There's one more thing I need to say,'' she whispered. "I had another name where I came from. But Max called me Annie. I'd like to keep that name now, if that's okay.''

Max's heart contracted. "Oh, yeah,'' he said. "I don't think anyone will object to that.''

Chapter Seventeen

Bert Trainer leaned against the trunk of a palm tree in a little park near the center of Sea Kingdom. From the shade, he watched the laughing, smiling people walk past him on the blacktop path.

He had a dull headache and he felt sick to his stomach, even with a double dose of antacids. But he was excited, too. After all these years, it was finally going to happen. His destiny was here. He had come to accept that. And he knew that he had to find Annie Oakland. Or whatever her name was.

His hand wasn't quite steady as he fingered the bulky knapsack he'd brought. Stroking the fabric made him feel better. He'd packed carefully and gotten into the park with the equipment he thought he'd need. But he didn't know how anything was going to turn out.

ANNIE STOOD STILL for a moment, looking around at the crowd that surged through Sea Kingdom. As soon as she had been fit to travel, she and twenty Light Street–Randolph Security volunteers had flown from Maryland to Florida. This time she'd been prepared for the experience of being high above the ground.

On the trip down, they'd looked at videos of the

theme park and made plans. Then they'd driven immediately to the park to familiarize themselves with the layout. After that, they'd gone to a nearby hotel for a planning meeting. They were as prepared as they could be, in so short a time.

Under protest, Katie had given Annie a stimulant. Still, Annie felt barely competent to carry out her assignment as she walked through the vast park. The governor was giving his speech in about an hour. And Charles Carpenter was here, too. Her awareness of him threatened to choke off her breath.

She felt as if she was drowning out in the open air, surrounded by families with laughing children.

The sparkling landscape and the press of people were almost too much for her. She had never in her life seen so much wide-open space and so many people. Happy, carefree people. They were all around her, smiling and eating and enjoying the attractions—and they didn't know how near they were to death.

She could feel that death—so close, like huge, black vultures circling over the landscape.

And she could feel Charles Carpenter. He was breathing the same air that she breathed. Moving through the same happy throngs.

And she had to find him. Before it was too late.

She had described him to the Light Street team as best she could. Some of them were in the auditorium, trying to spot the terrorist among the crowd. But there were no photographs of the man, only an artist's rendition that made him look like the devil incarnate. There'd been no way to trace him; Charles Carpenter wasn't his real name.

Feeling as if someone was staring at her back, she swung around to look over her shoulder. Could Carpenter be somewhere behind her? Could he know that she—or someone like her—was looking for him?

No one met his description that she could see. Her senses told her she was moving toward him, so she kept walking along a blacktop path past a pond colorful with water fowl.

In these throngs of people, without the touchstone, finding Carpenter would have been an impossible task. She'd had no idea how big this place was, because nothing in her experience had prepared her for the endless park or the blue dome of sky overhead. But the special cells the Handlers had grafted into her were guiding her to him.

Her heart rate picked up, and her hands began to tremble. Now she was sure she was closing in on him. Proximity was making her sick and shaky and so full of tension she felt as if a live electrical wire was sizzling through her.

Gritting her teeth, she focused on the crowd, scanning faces, thinking that looking for Carpenter was like looking for a grain of food in a chemical dump. But at least Carpenter was alone. Then again, he could have brought along a decoy family to make him less suspicious. She'd heard of terrorists who'd done that. But was Carpenter that *sick?*

She stumbled over uneven blacktop and caught herself.

Twenty yards away, she saw Max start toward her, but she shook her head. She didn't want him beside her. She didn't want him at the center of danger. But he had insisted on keeping her in sight.

He had come down here with the Light Street volunteers. If she thought about what they were doing, she would start to choke up. More people than they needed had asked to be part of this mission. If she failed, everybody who had come down here with her could die. She prayed Thorn could save them. He had used the antibodies in her blood to make a serum that would counteract the virus. The trouble was, there'd been no way to test it yet.

Annie clenched her fists, then deliberately forced her hands to relax. There was no way she could have made it this far by herself. Maybe that was why the other time travelers had failed. The Handlers had wanted the mission to be secret at all costs. But they had no idea what someone coming from the future would face.

An impossible task. The only reason she had gotten this far was thanks to Max and her other new friends. Max and the Randolph Security–Light Street team were making it possible for her to function.

She slid him a quick, grateful look, and he gave her a thumbs-up. She smiled and signaled back.

Last night she'd made love with him, and it had been glorious. She'd never imagined such joy in her life. If she could sleep in his arms for the next hundred years, that would be heaven. But she couldn't see past this day, this moment—because she was prepared to do whatever it would take to stop the man who had turned her world into a living hell.

Max thought he knew what was at stake. But he hadn't lived in the disaster zone that had become the planet Earth. He didn't know what it was like to live in an environment that was raw and harsh and soul-destroying. Where every imaginable environmental disaster, including nuclear bombs, had made large areas uninhabitable. Where living outside a complex took decades off your life, if you survived past childhood.

All that had made the men and women who had

trained her for this mission fanatical. They were brittle, nasty people. When she thought about Angelo, the head of the project, she started to tremble. He had sent her here to die. He hadn't cared about her. But that wasn't surprising. Where she came from, human life was cheap. There were too many people for the resources they had left. And too much effort had to be put into making the underground environment habitable.

"You okay?" Max asked through her special cell phone. He and the other Randolph Security agents who were fanned out around the park were all hooked to the same network, so they could hear one another.

"No," she said. It was difficult to speak, difficult just to breathe. Carpenter was too close now. She knew that from the touchstone the Handlers had put inside her. As she took a path that led past the dolphin tanks toward the penguin house, the pain in her head worsened.

She thought about what the Handlers had told her. They'd said the touchstone would lead her to Carpenter. They hadn't told her the damn thing would make her so sick. Maybe they hadn't known the effect or maybe they had put too much of it into her body to make sure she could find him.

Where was Carpenter? When was he going to release the virus? She didn't know the answer to either question. But she had to stop him.

Her task would have been easier if she had a gun. But with the security measures in place after 9-11, she would have been taking a chance trying to get a weapon into the park. If caught, she would have been hauled away by the police and had no chance at Carpenter.

A sudden pain stabbed her head.

"He's close," she whispered into her phone. "Very

close. I guess he isn't going to the place where the governor is speaking."

"We'll zero in on your position." It was Jed who answered.

The people around her were a blur of sound and movement.

Ahead of her was a bed of bright orange and yellow flowers. A pity she didn't know their name, she thought. But there had been no room for such luxuries in her dark, barren world.

As she marveled that anyone would put so much effort into a flower bed, a maintenance man in a green uniform stopped a small truck near the display.

She looked from the flowers to the vehicle. She'd seen trucks like it in the park earlier. The sign on the side indicated they were used for spraying insecticide.

The driver walked to the back of the vehicle and unhooked a hose. And as he pulled it toward the yellow and orange flowers, pain grabbed her by the throat, almost knocking her to her knees.

In that instant, she *knew*.

It was he. Carpenter. A man with brown hair, dark eyes and pale skin. Not Satan. A normal-looking man in a green uniform.

With a sick certainty, she knew that the virus was in the truck's tank unit, and he was getting ready to spray it into the air. And everybody in the park was going to get the deadly infection.

"It's him!" she shouted as she ran toward the truck. From her right she saw another body hurtling toward her.

The man's face swam into focus, and she gasped. It was Sheriff Bert Trainer. He was running toward her. He was going to stop her.

No! Not Trainer. Not now. What the carp was he doing here? How had he known where to find her? They had told her someone would try to stop her, and now she knew it was true.

Max saw him, too, and came running. "Get out of the way," Trainer screamed as he hurled himself forward. "Let me do my job."

Just before Trainer reached her, Max grabbed the man. Trainer bellowed and tried to throw him off, but Max pulled him to the ground where they began to struggle. Trainer fought like a madman, trying to get to her. All because she'd broken up his drug ring?

Annie saw the fight only from the corner of her eye. She kept moving, struggling against the awful pain coursing through her as she ran toward Carpenter. She felt as if she was swimming through poisonous water, choking, gasping, and she was sure she couldn't get there in time.

When Carpenter looked up and saw her, his face went pale with shock, and she realized then that he'd had no idea anyone might be here to interfere with him.

"Get away!" he screamed, then he quickly turned and reached for the hose controls.

Passersby froze in surprise, riveted to a drama they couldn't understand.

Miraculously, Annie reached Carpenter, tearing him away from the hose handle, flinging him against the side of the truck. He lunged for her, and they struggled. He was strong and desperate; she was so sick she could barely fight him. It was only because Katie had given her a stimulant that she had any chance at all. But finally, inevitably, he wrenched himself away.

Desperately, she made another grab for him, her fingers tangling in his shirt. With a low growl like a wounded animal, he turned and clawed at her.

Then someone else was beside her. She saw Jason throwing the mass murderer to the ground and follow him down. But was it already too late? She heard a hissing noise. The virus. Was it in the hose or in the tank?

Maybe she could still stop the horror. At least she had to try.

Expecting at every moment that Carpenter would leap on her again, she reached to turn the valve back to the off position. The metal handle wouldn't move. Panic roaring in her ears, she pushed harder, and the lever gave. As it did, the hissing noise stopped, and she breathed out a sigh of profound relief.

Blinking, she looked at the hose lying limply on the ground.

A scream from behind her made her turn. In their struggle, Jason had thrown Carpenter against a metal fence where he lay panting. Randolph agents moved to block her view, but she heard one of the men on the ground curse.

"What?" she gasped. "Is he getting away?"

"Not likely," Steve answered, coming toward her. "The bastard had a cyanide capsule under the front of his shirt collar. He's dead."

She slumped against the truck. She should have realized that he was no longer living. The touchstone had gone cold inside her. Probably if the tiny computer was still under her skin, she would have fallen down dead, too. And then it would have destroyed itself, so no one would know.

But that didn't happen. She had stopped Carpenter, and she was still alive.

She couldn't quite believe what had happened. Had she and the Randolph agents really changed history? Had they prevented Charles Carpenter from turning the world into a wasteland?

"Annie. Over here, Annie. Quick."

Disoriented, she pushed away from the truck and saw Max motioning to her as he crouched over Trainer.

She sucked in a breath when she realized she'd been so focused on her mission she'd forgotten about the sheriff.

Hurrying to Max, she knelt beside the man on the ground. His breath was ragged.

"What's wrong?" she asked.

He didn't answer the question. "I didn't come…to hurt you. I came to help."

Annie struggled to rearrange her thinking. "Why?"

"Angelo sent you…didn't he?" he asked.

She stared at the man. "How do you know?"

"He…sent me. Thirty years too…early. At first I didn't remember why I was…here. Then I remembered…but I knew I had to wait."

He was silent for several moments, his breath rattling in his chest. With a wheezing cough, he began to speak again. "I guess…I convinced myself it wasn't…going to happen. Till you…" He coughed again, and she could see he was in bad shape. "I got to live here…for thirty years. I was…cop back home. Here, too." He coughed again. "What's…wrong with me?"

"The tattoo under your arm, it's got poison. It's set to go into your system after you finish your assignment."

He made a dry, rattling sound. "Angelo…bastard."

"Yes," she said past a tight throat.

"I saw your notes...in boat. I...had to...come here. Then I...felt Carpenter..."

"With your touchstone," she concluded for him. "I guess it lost a lot of its power—until you got close to him."

"Saw...you...and..." His voice trailed off, and he lay with his eyes closed. "You got him. Thank God." Those were his last words.

Annie stared at the man who had enjoyed terrorizing her that night on the dock. "He was nasty, like them," she said to Max. "But he came here to do what he was trained to do. Like me."

"Yeah," Max replied. "He had all the makings for a hard-assed cop. All he had to do was learn to speak Southern. But in the end, he came through for your Handlers."

Max helped her up and took her in his arms. "It's over. It's all over." He stroked his hands over her back, her shoulders.

Behind him she could see someone had slapped a Poison sign on the truck. Beside it, Jason was talking to the police.

"I have to—"

Max interrupted her. "You have to do nothing. It's finished. You can go on with your life. No thanks to Angelo."

"But I should talk to the police."

"No. Jason will handle it. He's got evidence that Light Street learned about the plot from another source. You don't have to get involved at all."

She blinked up at him, trying to take it in. It was difficult to wrap her mind around the truth, but finally she said, "I guess I don't."

"It's over for you," he said, his tone firm. "You've done enough."

"Did I change history? Is my world different?"

"From the way you described it, I hope so."

There was something she'd been worrying about for the past two days. "Then why am I still here?" she asked in a voice she couldn't quite keep steady.

He stared at her, then cursed. "I didn't think about that. I guess your damn Handlers didn't, either, if they decided they had to kill you. Or maybe they know something we don't." He stopped and ran a shaky hand through his hair. "Do you remember your life? Where you came from?"

She thought about it. Her memories had been sharp and clear until a few minutes ago. Now what she remembered was hazy, like a bad dream from which she'd awakened. "I don't know," she whispered. "Ask me later."

He held her tightly as though he feared she might vanish. And she held him just as frantically. But as the seconds ticked by and she didn't fade away, she began to relax. Something had happened. The world had changed. But she hadn't disappeared from existence.

She let Max draw her into a little courtyard, where they were sheltered by stone walls. Bright purple flowers cascaded around them.

In an alcove, water spouted from the mouth of a stone fish into a basin that sparkled in the sunlight.

She looked around in wonder, breathing in the fragrance from the flowers. "It's so beautiful here."

He turned her toward him, then bent to brush his lips against hers. The gentle kiss made her heart feel light. Lifting his head again, he looked down at her and smiled. "Yes. This is a good place for me to ask you to marry me."

She stared at him. "You want to...to marry me?" she asked.

"Yes. I knew it that first night we made love in Maryland. I should have told you then. I should have told you how much I love you."

"It wouldn't have changed my decision," she heard herself say. "I would still have had to come here today. And you would have been angrier at me than you already were."

He laughed. "Yeah, you've got that right. But you were persistent. You would have made me understand why it was important to get that bastard out there." He gestured over his shoulder.

She licked her suddenly dry lips. "I had to try to stop him. I would have come here by myself."

"I know."

"So that makes me like your wife—the woman who was killed."

He shook his head. "You're not like her. She had to keep proving herself over and over. And she went off on one too many dangerous missions. You didn't have anything to prove. You knew you had something vitally important to do, even when you couldn't remember what it was."

"Because I had that thing planted under my skin."

"That wasn't the only reason, and you know it. Your sense of purpose didn't go away after I took it out. When you remembered what was going to happen to the world, you knew you had to stop Carpenter."

"Yes. But the Handlers didn't understand that I could only do it with your help. Thank you, Max. Thank you for letting me come here. I know how hard that was for you."

"Yeah." He hugged her close. "And thank you for bringing me back to life. Thank you for making me care about someone again. I was operating on automatic pilot until I hooked up with you."

"Oh, Max." She drew back her head to look into his face. "I never thought I could love anyone. I mean…well, I loved my mother. She was a wonderful person, even in our world. She gave me a good start in life. But we weren't allowed to…get involved with anyone. Women and men lived in separate dormers."

"You got involved with me pretty quickly."

She felt a flush heat her face. "I'd never met anyone like you. You weren't harsh and mean. Even when you were furious with me, you were gentle."

"By your standards, I guess." He cleared his throat, looking anxious. "So why don't you give me an answer to the question I asked?"

She felt the tension in him, felt her own heart start to pound. "Maybe I can never fit in here," she whispered.

"People are resilient. You've already proved that." He gave her a direct look. "You and I are going to be a very, very good team. Unless you're too scared to take a chance on happiness."

She *was* scared. She had never thought that she could have any of the good things that he and his friends took for granted. But her universe had expanded since the moment he had pulled her out of the river.

She took a breath and let it out. "Max, I love you."

"Thank God."

"But you're taking on a lot with me."

"Let me worry about that."

Part of her wanted to keep arguing, and part of her wanted to lose herself in his arms. It was the latter impulse that won, because she let her heart rule her head. "I'll marry you," she said.

"Oh, honey. Thank you!" He squeezed her so hard she could barely breathe.

Then he lowered his mouth, taking hers in a deep, passionate kiss that left her breathless. It was broad daylight. They were in a courtyard where anyone could walk in and see them. And they were kissing. But there was nothing wrong with it. Nothing wrong with their being together. Not in this world.

"Max," she murmured, "I never even knew a man like you could exist."

He stroked her back as he replied, "I don't know exactly what kind of man I am, but being with you makes me better than I was."

"That's true for me, too," she whispered. "But, Max…"

"What?"

She was almost afraid to say the next words. "You told me about your family."

"And?"

"Can we…can I have your children? And can all of us live together?"

"Oh, yes. But first give yourself a little while to get used to living in this world." He knit her fingers with his. "I suggest we get out of here. If we're lucky, we can sneak off to our hotel room for a couple of hours. I'll tell everyone you need to rest." His wicked look told her that rest wasn't exactly what he had in mind.

She grinned back, finally daring to let happiness bloom within her as Max led her out of the courtyard and into the rest of their lives.

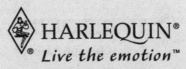

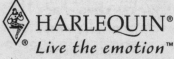

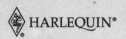
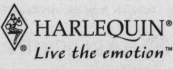